I0729216

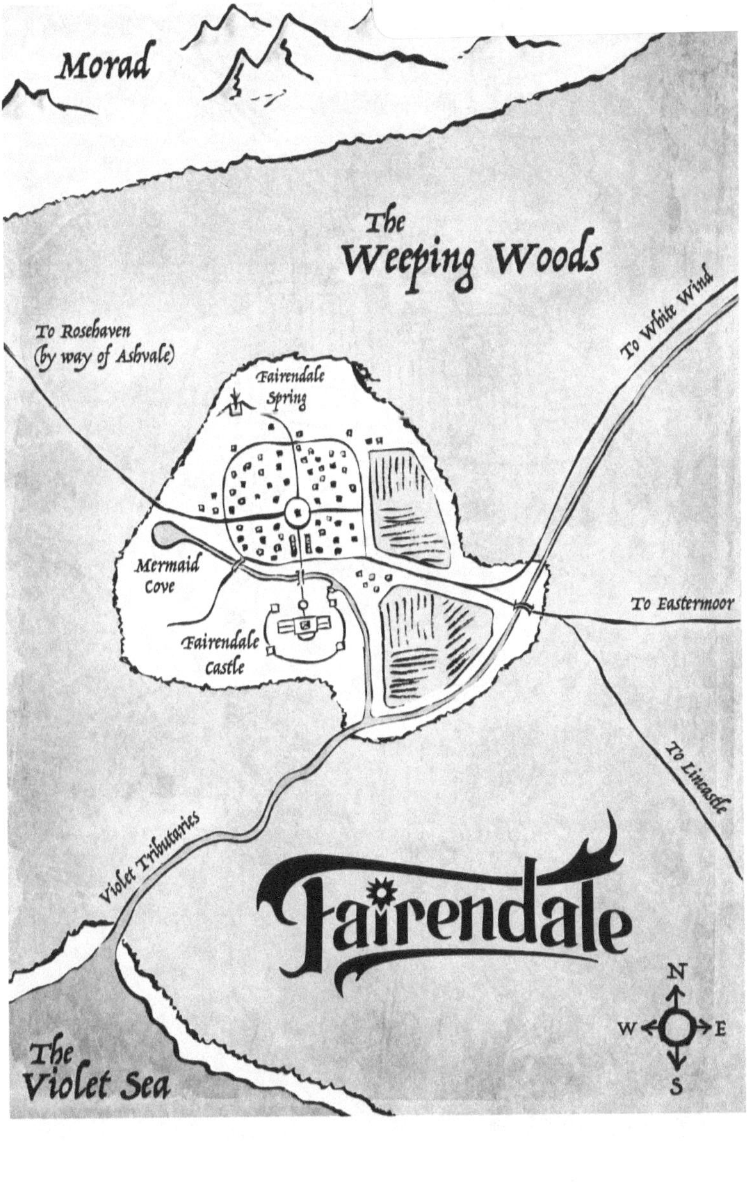

Morad
The Weeping Woods
To Rosehaven
(by way of Ashvale)
To White Wind
Fairendale Spring
Mermaid Cove
To Eastermoor
Fairendale Castle
To Lincastle
Violet Tributaries
Fairendale
The Violet Sea
N
W
E
S

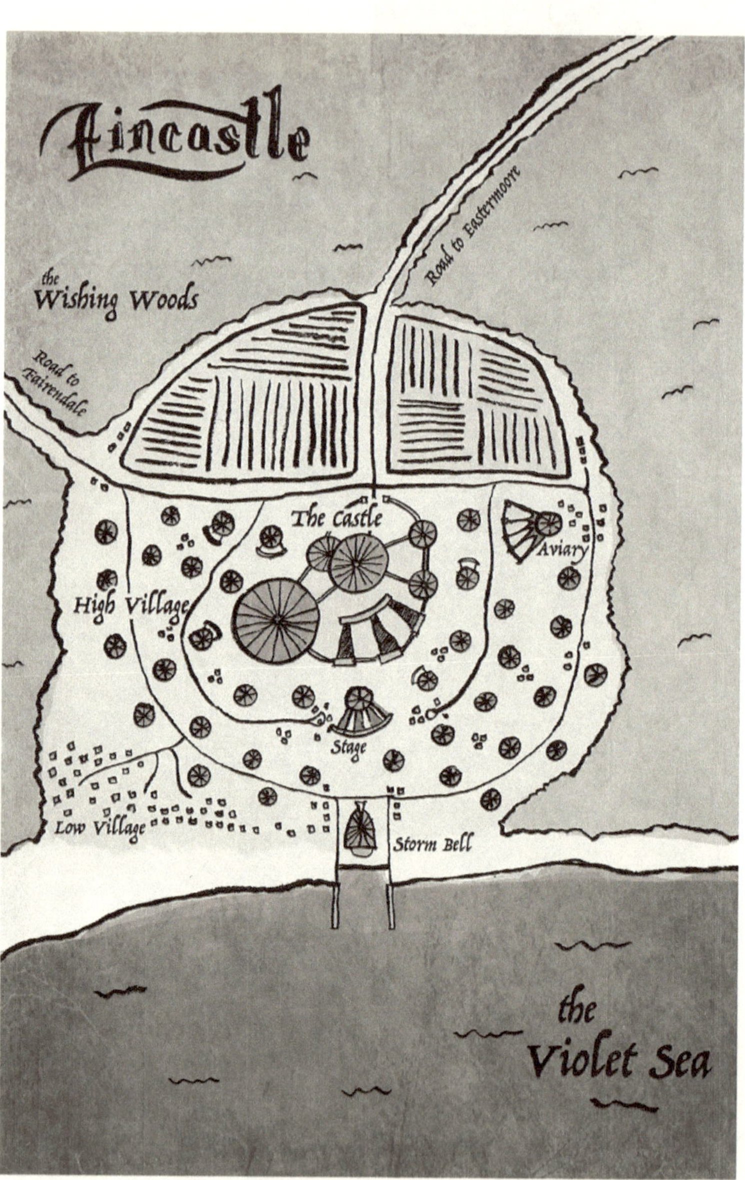

Fincastle
the Wishing Woods
Road to Eastermoor
Road to Fairendale
The Castle
Aviary
High Village
Stage
Low Village
Storm Bell
the Violet Sea

Fairendale

15

THE BOY WHO
FRIGHTENED
MISS MUFFET

Read all the books in the Fairendale series!

Collector's Editions:

To see all the books L.R. Patton has written, please click or visit the link below:

www.lrpatton.com/writing

L.R. PATTON
THE BOY WHO FRIGHTENED MISS MUFFET
BATLEE PRESS

Published by
Batlee Press
Post Office Box 591596
San Antonio, TX 78259

The author appreciates your taking the time to read her work. Please consider leaving a review wherever you bought it and telling your friends how much you enjoyed it. Both of those help get the book into the hands of new readers, which is incredibly important for authors. Thank you for your support.
www.lrpatton.com

Names: Patton, L.R., author.
Title: The boy who frightened miss muffet / L.R. Patton
Description: First edition. | Batlee Press, Texas: Batlee Press Books, 2019

10 9 8 7 6 5 4 3 2 1

First Edition—2019

For those who are misunderstood
and most in need of the question
why
and the assurance that
you are loved

Choices

The Enchantress of Fairendale stares into a magical looking ball, which turns her face a luminous shade of green. What she sees within it startles her so powerfully that she lets out a strangled cry.

The Huntsman, with whom she travels to collect all the lost children of Fairendale who fled during an invasion of the king's men nearly two moons ago (she collects them for unknown purposes but, presumably, to hand over to the king of Fairendale), is by her side in a moment.

"What is it?" he says.

She has let the ball go dark. She presses a hand against her mouth. Her heart pounds.

She has seen—what has she seen? The next child? Impossible. It was an enormous spider.

Enormous on the looking ball or enormous in reality? The Enchantress shudders. No, she saw the trees. These spiders are almost as tall as the trees, which makes them…

Monsters. Nightmares. Inconceivably awful.

"What have you seen?" the Huntsman persists.

The Enchantress shakes her head and points to the ball. The Huntsman says, "I cannot see anything."

Oh. Yes. She must call up the vision again. She does not want to. Her mouth feels dry, her hands clammy. But she swallows hard and raises her hands slightly above the ball. It glows to life, and there is the hideous vision again. She casts her eyes to the ground.

The Huntsman sucks in a breath. "What…?" The Huntsman tilts his head. The Enchantress watches him rather than the ball. "What is that?"

"I believe they call that a monster," the Enchantress says. She tries with all her might to maintain her dignity and keep her voice steady. But it slips, falters, snags in her throat.

The Enchantress and the Huntsman are camped outside the land of Eastermoor, where they have successfully captured the latest lost child of Fairendale. She, a magical girl, joins all the others. These captives are no longer children, they are blackbirds, kept in iron cages, arranged in a line inside a cart pulled by a white mare. There should be seven birds, but four days ago the Enchantress and the Huntsman woke from a malodorous (which is to say, smelly) encounter with a Bonnacon to find one of the blackbirds missing. They have not formally discussed him. Not yet. They have only talked around him a time or two.

There is a good line of tension hardening between the two of them. The Enchantress, in their quest, has faithfully followed the lead of this magical looking ball, but it only shows one Fairendale child at a time. The Huntsman does not trust the ball. Neither knows whether the magical orb will show them again the child they have already found and subsequently lost.

So, rather than discuss the looking ball's merits or failures, they simply ignore them.

But now there is this: a spider. Days ago, they were shown (and retrieved, by a great stroke of luck) an egg.

"How could a child become a monstrous spider after a Vanishing spell?" the Huntsman says. He shakes his head.

Spider. The word echoes in the Enchantress's head. She never could abide spiders. In fact, it was the one thing that could clear her from a room faster than anything else. She would not even kill them. And if a spider crawled across a room and disappeared beneath a chair, the Enchantress would refuse to sit on that chair ever after.

And now they must capture an oversized one. She does not know how she will conceal her fear—this weakness—from the Huntsman.

A large, sharp-toothed wolf she could take. But a spider?

Perhaps the ball is mocking her. She scowls at it, but the spiders in it begin to move. She closes her eyes and presses her fingers against them.

She can feel the eyes of the Huntsman warming her face. She blinks. The ball is dark, the vision gone. Good. Her eyes lift to the Huntsman's. He seems to be asking something.

The lost child?

"The ball has never been wrong," the Enchantress says. It is what she always says. She has not enough strength or stamina to discuss this right now. If it is a trap, she will walk right into it.

But with spiders?

Without a word, both their eyes move to the dragon egg lodged between two cages. *That* vision might have been wrong, but the egg has not hatched, and there is no way to know.

Do they follow on blind faith, or do they try to continue on their own? The question has been growing larger of late.

A blackbird twitters. The Enchantress sighs.

"Well," the Huntsman says, but he says no more. He drops beside her on the ground. After a time, during which both of them stare at nothing, he says, "I hope he is a friendly spider."

The Enchantress clears her throat but remains silent.

"A Vanishing spell is complicated," the Huntsman says. "It could have gone wrong."

"A Vanishing spell can do whatever it likes," the Enchantress says. "There is always some risk. They might not have reappeared at all."

The Huntsman brightens. "Could we not tell the king that they all vanished and did not reappear?"

It seems like a simple solution. But the Enchantress knows that there is rarely a simple solution to anything. She says, "Do you think the boy who has been turned into a spider would like to remain a spider?" Frederick is his name. The ball said as much, along with his location: Lincastle. They have traveled to Lincastle twice already.

The words of the Enchantress hang between them.

At last the Huntsman says, "No, I do not think he would."

And who would?

The Huntsman takes a breath. "But what if—"

"Enough, Huntsman." The Enchantress's voice is sharp and low. She is not in the mood for questioning. She grows more and more weary by the day, and she would like to finish this quest as soon as possible. Fourteen children remain at large, excepting the giant spider. She does not count the other two she knows about; she also does not count the dragon egg. How could a child become a dragon, folded up in an egg? It is impossible, even for magic.

She and the Huntsman are not even halfway finished with their quest. Her eyes burn thinking about it.

If the ball would show them more than one child at a time, how much more quickly they could do this! The anger is fierce and hot, but the Enchantress swallows it down. It would not do for her to show the Huntsman how much she agrees with him.

Into the quiet, the Huntsman says, "How could a Vanishing spell accomplish something like this?"

The Enchantress shakes her head. She does not know. So all she says is, "It must have been a strong spell." And well it must, to have taken twenty-two children and spread them throughout the seven kingdoms, utterly changed from their original forms.

Except Oscar. He remained the same. Perhaps there are more like him, still the same children they were before.

The Enchantress glares at the looking ball. She wishes she could coax it to show her everyone. She could better conserve her magic, better lay out the plans, better strategize if it did. She would have control. She never liked not being in control.

The Huntsman disturbs her thoughts. "Does anyone have magic this strong in the land of Fairendale?" he says.

"Some."

The Huntsman is quiet only for a moment. "You," he says.

Yes, she almost agrees, but something about his voice —a tiny note of suspicion—stops her. She raises her chin and looks directly at him. "I am not responsible for this spell."

He looks at her for a long time. She looks back. She wants him to know that she is telling the truth. She wants him to know that he can trust her.

Why is it so important to have his trust? The Enchantress cannot answer this.

After a time, the Huntsman casts his eyes to the forest floor and nods. His voice is quiet when he says, "Do you think you will be able to turn them back into children? Do you think you have that kind of power?"

What he is asking is more complicated than it sounds. The rules of a Vanishing spell say that one can only become someone different once in their lifetime. You vanish, and you become someone—or something—else. Sometimes you do not reappear at all. It is always a risk in spells where magic has the upper hand, which is the case with a Vanishing spell. It is very dark magic.

But the rules have been bent, it seems. The Enchantress, upon finding the children in their new forms, has been able to turn them into blackbirds. She does not understand it, which means she does not know how to answer the Huntsman's question. It is not the first time he has asked. And it is likely not the last.

It *is* the first time that she tells him the truth. "I do not know."

The Huntsman nods again, as though this is what he expected.

"I wonder how he feels about being a monster," the Huntsman says.

The Enchantress shudders. "It cannot be enjoyable."

"Do you think he knows he is a monster?"

"Does anyone?" The Enchantress does not mean for the words to come out, but they are stronger than her will. She feels the eyes of the Huntsman on her again, but she does not meet them, and he does not answer.

They are quiet again until she says, "Do you think we will be able to save him?"

"What do you mean?"

"I mean, he is a spider. Perhaps it is too dangerous." She means she does not want to do this.

"We cannot leave him there."

No. He is right. And, besides, the looking ball will not show them the next child until this one has been successfully collected. So she says, "Well. I suppose we should rest before beginning our travels." She will need days of rest to deal with enormous spiders. But she does not say this aloud; she does not like exposing weakness to the Huntsman.

The Huntsman nods. His eyes are a glassy blue.

The Enchantress stands. "I will leave you to feed the children."

The Huntsman looks up at her in surprise. She knows why. Most nights she calls them birds, not children. Well, perhaps this quest has changed her a bit. Let him wonder at that.

With a whisper of her dress, she moves past him and toward her tent. She does not look back, though she can feel his eyes fastened on her, following her. A smile tugs at the corners of her lips.

When she has reached her tent, she lets it win.

In another forest entirely, some distance from where the Enchantress and the Huntsman camp for the evening, is an old crone with silvery hair and milky eyes, looking in a ball of her own. It is perfectly circular and small enough to slide into a pocket of her ragged dress. She holds it in a hand of bones—bones so old they look as though they might break if she were to straighten any of the bent fingers that curl around the ball. Her eyes rove over a scene.

How can such an old woman with such milky eyes see what a looking ball of this size has to show her?

Well, magic is mysterious, dear reader. And this woman is not all she seems. She is in good company; there are many in this story who are much more than they seem.

In her tiny looking ball, the old crone—now with eyes sharpened by a color that could be called "sky at dusk"—sees the Enchantress, huddling over her green looking ball outside the village of Eastermoor. The crone waves one hand over her tiny ball, and the scene on the looking ball in front of the Enchantress shifts and changes. Now there is a spider. Now there is the word: Lincastle. Now there is a name: Frederick.

The old crone smiles, watches. For a moment, her figure flashes into that of a much younger woman—a woman with golden hair and a smooth face and wide, sapphire eyes. It happens so quickly that an observer might very well dismiss it as imagination, a trick of the eye. She is the old woman again, bent nearly in two.

Beside her, resting against the earth, is a staff of almond wood with iron claws that curl around nothing.

On her wrist is a dark brown bracelet with a sapphire jewel in the middle of it.

The woman now flips through several scenes: a tiny girl, a tiny boy, a sea witch, jester twins (she has plans for those two, plans they will enjoy.).

As she watches these children—some changed from their original forms, some unchanged completely—her face seems to grow darker. A coppery color. Is it the shadows of the woods that make her look as though she is the same old woman who once begged in the streets of Lincastle, who spoke to Philip, the lost child who became the leader of the merry men, stealing from the rich and giving to the poor? Or is it magic?

The old crone leans closer to her ball. The scene

before her shows the land of Guardia. There is a child here, yes—and something else.

Snow rising up from the ground.

Well, it is about time.

The old woman chuckles and coughs. A flicker, a shimmer, a straight and young form that fades back into this old one.

She turns to look at the way she came. She intended on returning to the house of the Enchantress and waking the woman and the child who sleep there—a mother and daughter, resting with the help of a Sleeping spell—but plans change. There is something else she must do now. She steels her courage, takes a deep breath, and vanishes in a cloud of rose-colored smoke.

This woman is a shape shifter—but an entirely different kind than we have met thus far. This woman is the kind of shape shifter who can put on any skin she likes. Beast, human, bird, wolf, they are nothing to her. She has been them all, and she will likely be them all again.

There is only one shape shifter of this kind who exists in the world.

The streets of Lincastle have grown chaotic in the last few days. Neighbor has turned against neighbor, families sit quietly at supper tables, the streets have all but emptied out. The weather, too, is out of sorts. In this tropical land, where no one owns anything warmer than a light cloak or robe, the sun has hidden of late, behind puffy gray clouds. The wind gusts through the streets, knocking hats from heads. The people shiver.

They argue and disagree and shout because not only did some kind of natural disturbance four days ago shake the very ground on which they walk, but the boy tasked with ringing the storm bell rang it, and the people huddled in their homes for hours, and no storm bludgeoned the land or their houses. They have practiced these Sea Storm Drills all their lives, but they did not think this was a drill. And the anger swells larger in them. And the fingers point sharper. And the looks turn distrustful.

Living in discord is not an enjoyable community life.

The spider, of course, does not know about all this. Frederick, one of the lost children of Fairendale who was transported to the land of Lincastle and (hideously, depending on how you feel about spiders) transformed into a gigantic spider, is only just now coming into his own consciousness, as that of a thinking and breathing and living arachnid. He is disturbed by what he senses he has become; people do not have as many legs as he has. People do not have fragmented eyesight, either. People do not have—what is that? Fangs?

Oh, mercy.

Frederick tries to breathe, not panic. His senses are alive; he feels every movement beneath this ground—is he beneath the ground? It does feel similar to when he and Arthur and Maude and the other lost children of Fairendale hid beneath the ground of the Weeping Woods, trying to avoid the king's men, who pursued him and all the other children, by order of the king of Fairendale, because of a magical boy.

Magic is dangerous in Fairendale, particularly for a male; it is the only requirement for becoming a king.

Frederick tries to move, but there is no moving; he is folded up into a ball, his legs—eight of them!—bent and creased. And there are others—oh! There are others! Inside the ball with him! Crawling all over him!

He will not scream. He will not scream. He will not scream.

He opens his mouth, but a scream does not pour forth.

This must be a nightmare. He closes his eyes, but there are too many! He cannot close them all. He still sees what he sees, shadowed but sharp. Wriggling legs and awful eyes and the kind of bodies that show up in only his worst imaginings.

He must get out. He cannot breathe. He presses his back—no, not his back, something else—into the sac. It is a sac. He can see its milky threads, light splintering between fibers.

Of all the things one might become because of a Vanishing spell, he had to become a spider? He could not even kill a spider when he was a boy; he was too terrified that it would jump on him as he raised a piece of parchment or a shoe to swat it.

Frederick feels sick to his stomach. He presses harder against the edge of the sac. The sooner he can break through it the sooner he will be able to escape. The sooner he will—what? Walk around Fairendale as a spider? How long would he last?

Frederick slumps to the pile beneath him—until he remembers what that pile is: spiders.

He resumes his frantic pressing, poking, breaking.

A muffled voice reaches him from outside the sac. A person? He can understand the speech. It must be, then.

Is it better or worse that a person is waiting for him?

The sac tears with a whispery sound. Frederick tumbles out with a pile of other...yes, they are spiders.

Which means he is…

It is as he feared.

With a feeling of exceeding queasiness, Frederick takes in his eight legs, tries to stand upon them and collapses, and examines his surroundings with the fragmented, black-and-white vision that is afforded him as a spider.

How did this happen?

Now his senses are on high alert as they ring out one call: Danger! Danger! Danger! This entire underground chamber is filled with spiders much larger than him.

"They have hatched," says a booming voice, and Frederick looks up to see the largest spider he has ever seen in his entire life. The spider smiles at him—can spiders smile? This one does. He knows this spider is female, though he cannot say how. Perhaps it is his arachnid intuition. The spider bends down. "Hello there," she says. "No need to be afraid."

The words are nothing to Frederick. Of course he will be afraid! He is surrounded by spiders! Spiders that talk!

Frederick's first, more rational, thought is one of escape, but with so many very large spiders watching him, he does not think it is the proper time. There will be other opportunities; he is small, they are large, and he will not be missed.

At least this is what he hopes.

His second thought is of equal weight: Where are the other children?

Where is Maude? Where is his mother? Why is he here?

He knows a little about Vanishing spells. He knows that one who undergoes a Vanishing spell may or may not return to the earth. He knows he is fortunate to have returned. But he is a spider. Is it fortunate or unfortunate? Would it have been better to disappear? Can he become himself again, after having lived as a spider?

And what if he dies as a spider? What then?

The large female spider leans close to him again. She says, "Welcome to the world, little spider. I am Demarek. I will look after you. I will keep you safe."

And for some reason the words, though they come from a spider who looks like Frederick imagines he will look when he is grown (and when will that be? Will he make it to adulthood as a spider? Does he want to? There are so many questions that cannot be answered, and Frederick has never liked questions that could not be answered), he feels comforted by them. He feels warm. Secure. As long as he is with Demarek, can anything hurt him?

Another large spider ambles toward Frederick. He can see that some small spiders have crawled onto this one's back. Frederick remains where he is, cowering near Demarek.

"Go on," Demarek says gently. "She is your mother."

And Frederick would like to say that no, she is not, she is nothing of the sort. He has a mother, and he left her and his father and his older sister, who was getting married next month (though perhaps the month has already passed; he must have spent a little time in the spider sac). This is not his place. This is not his family. This is not his life.

She pushes him forward.

"What is wrong with him?" The booming voice returns, and there is a spider even larger than Demarek and Frederick's spider mother. Frederick makes a hissing sound, and fear wraps around him like another egg sac.

"Nothing is wrong with him," Demarek says. "He is just like the others. Eight legs, eight eyes, spider sense."

The largest spider moves closer. Frederick's hissing turns into a screech that sounds like a whispery whistle.

He did not even know spiders could make a noise like this one. He has learned something today.

He would rather not have.

"Your noise," the large spider says in a voice that seems to shake the cavern or the hole or wherever it is they are.

"Sparso." Demarek raises her voice only slightly, but there is a warning in it. "He is a hatchling."

"Your noise is intolerable," says Sparso. "See that he remains quiet, Demarek."

Frederick continues to hiss, though he wills himself to stop. It is as though he cannot control it. He looks at Demarek, who says, "Perhaps if you could say something to him, Sparso. Make him feel welcome."

The large spider turns all eight black eyes on Frederick. He says, "You do not climb up the abdomen of your mother, as all the rest do." He blinks, one eye at a time, like a wave of lids.

Frederick did not know spiders had lids on their eyes. Perhaps these are a special kind of spider. Or perhaps things are different when you become one.

Sparso continues. "He will be dead in a day."

Frederick shivers.

"Go on," Demarek whispers. "Climb onto your mother."

But she is not his mother, and he cannot claim it. So he remains where he is. And Sparso turns away. "Get him out of here, Demarek."

Frederick does not care. He would like very much to get out of here. Not on his spider-mother's back. Not on her abdomen. Not clinging to her legs. Nowhere near her, thank you.

Demarek glances at the spider-mother, who looks at Frederick and turns away. Demarek says, "Spider babies are supposed to be quiet. Unless you want to be eaten by your own father." She nods toward Sparso.

Frederick would like to say *He is not my father, he is not anything close to my father, my father would never ever, ever threaten to eat me because of the noise I was making.* But, of course, he keeps his words tucked away, for another time and place, or perhaps never.

If he ever escapes from this place, he will have quite a story to tell.

Frederick's chest aches. His father was the historian of Fairendale; he kept detailed records about everything. What will his father write about the day all the children disappeared from the village? Does his father know that he is here, that he is hidden where the king will never find him, that he is somewhat safe (though can one ever be safe in a den full of spiders?)? And is this safety worth it?

The faces of his father, his mother, and his sister haunt his mind. The safety of their home; the nourishment of their meals, though small; the familiarity of his father's voice, reading from a new historical text he penned: he misses it all.

He hopes with all his heart that he will someday make it back to them.

That he will someday be a boy and not a spider.

Demarek interrupts his thoughts with a "Come with me."

She takes large steps toward an opening flanked by spiders that look as though they are standing at attention. Frederick feels very small next to them.

When they have passed through the opening, Demarek whispers, "You are not like the others. I knew it immediately. But I believe you will live."

And for a moment, her eyes are not black but a piercing, wild blue.

Frederick stares, but the moment is gone, as though it were another part of his imagination. Frederick tries to keep up with Demarek; she is very fast. And Frederick walks with a limp. He has walked with a limp since he was three years old. His mother, then, warned him not to stand too close to the oven. But Frederick had always been too interested in fire, and he stood too close, and he burned the back of his leg badly—so badly, in fact, that the village Healer could not heal it completely. The muscle shortened, which led to his limp.

This limp is the only thing that reminds him that he is still himself, Frederick, a boy from the land of Fairendale. He limps, as a spider, with the third leg on his right side; as a boy he limped with his one and only right leg. He can remember the fire, the burn, the Healer's touch, even. He tucks the memory away, willing himself to always remember. He must remember he is a boy, not a spider, no matter what happens in the next several days or weeks or months or…

He will escape. He must.

After some minutes of walking (Frederick is already tired, but he would never say so), Frederick uses his voice and is surprised that words come out. "Where am I?" he says.

"We are underground, in the Cavern of Cerata," Demarek says.

"Why is my vision the way it is?" Frederick says.

"You mean shadowy and void of color?" Demarek says. She does not wait for him to answer. "Spiders do not see in color. They see only black and white. In fact, we do not see anything all that well. We rely on touch and vibration mostly." She takes a few more steps and says, "I am sure you can see better than most, however."

He does not ask her why. He already knows—and it is clear that she does, too.

"And who are you?" Frederick says.

Demarek stops, which gives Frederick a bit of time to catch up. She smiles again—spiders *can* smile. He has learned something else today. "I am your sister, Princess Demarek of Cerata."

A spider princess. He had no idea such a world existed.

"Welcome to your spider world," Demarek says. And the way she says it makes Frederick think that perhaps she, too, is something more than she seems.

It will be good to have some company here in this strange and terrifying world.

The king of Lincastle is angry. He has been angry for many days—six of them, to be exact. His daughter, Princess Freya, has disappeared, and he has good reason to believe it is because of the orders that came from King Willis of Fairendale—orders that say every child in every land must be turned over to him.

King Owen is going to retaliate; the king of Fairendale has gone too far this time. King Owen loves his daughter; he would do anything for her.

Even start a war.

He has made his plans, but a wise woman (his mother) once told him that a man should never execute plans while he feels angry. So King Owen has spent the last six days breathing, calming himself, waiting to see if his daughter turns up.

But she is still missing, he is still angry, and the king of Fairendale still insists on having the children.

As soon as King Owen discovered that his daughter was missing—which was by letter, from his wife, Queen Sophia, who informed him that his Head Regent, Von Albeck, planned to capture his daughter and trade her for a reward but did not succeed because his daughter had fled (good for her!)—he returned from his own quest to smooth over relations with the other kingdoms and discuss what could be done about a corrupt king on the throne that rules all the lands. His daughter's safety took precedence, and upon return, King Owen ordered Von Albeck into the dungeons and sent men to search for Princess Freya.

The search came up empty, except for the village bookseller, who babbled about the princess turning into a swan and a thief who stole from his bookshop, turned into a blackbird, and a powerful sorceress with flaming red hair.

There was nothing or no one to corroborate the

man's strange tales, so King Owen threw him, too, into the dungeons. He visits the man every day, to ask once more where Princess Freya is. Every day he asks, the bookseller tells King Owen that Princess Freya is a swan.

King Owen shakes his head. He cannot ask his men to find a swan; they would believe him mad. And, besides, Lincastle is full of them.

On the third day the bookseller told him this story, King Owen summoned the village Healer, who said that the poor man likely suffered a breakdown of some sort, perhaps from spending so much time with books and not people. King Owen dismissed the Healer as yet another fool from the village. Books did not make madmen; not reading them did!

There are many of them, it seems—fools, that is. But not all the people are fools. Some had come to see him in the days since Princess Freya disappeared. Some had come to leave their regrets, but others had come to pledge their allegiance.

They would fight, too, they said. They would like to keep their own children safe and sound.

The king paces back and forth in his throne room. Back and forth and back and forth. His heels click against the marble floor. His bronze jeweled throne gleams in the light streaming in from the walls of windows. He has always preferred the light, and it is rare that the heavy blue curtains are closed in this room.

As he paces, King Owen thinks. He thinks about what his mother taught him all those years ago. For anger to be the best catalyst, it must be the right anger: the kind of anger focused on justice. On giving people what they need. On making the world better.

What would make this world in which he lives better?

King Owen turns and paces the length of the throne room again.

This time he thinks of what his queen told him this morning: His people—his people!—are searching for any and all children—their children! They have grown greedy in their pursuit of riches. They will trade the lives and safety and wellbeing of children for lives of wealth and privilege and supremacy.

Not in his kingdom.

Not his daughter.

Not the sons and daughters of those he respects.

Not innocent children.

Since he can no longer trust his three regents, after Von Albeck's betrayal, King Owen sends for the captain of his king's guard, Sir Maurius, who is usually at guard outside the door of whatever room King Owen inhabits.

The captain bows low when he enters the king's

presence. He is a man about the same age as King Owen. They have known each other since they were children; Sir Maurius's father served King Owen's father on the throne, as his grandfather also served King Owen's grandfather. The king's guard has been in the hands of Sir Maurius's family for generations.

King Owen knows he can trust this man.

"There is no word of your daughter, sire," Sir Maurius says, his hands gripping one another.

King Owen shakes his head. "I have summoned you for something else." He pauses, then says, "The time has come."

Sir Maurius fixes his soft brown eyes on his king, and, after a moment, nods once. "Would you like some parchment and a pen?"

"Please," King Owen says. "It will be faster than a visit."

Sir Maurius bows again. "I will send in the page."

"But first," King Owen says, and the captain turns on his heel to face his king again.

"Yes, sire?" Sir Maurius says.

"We will expect a war," King Owen says. His voice is strong and sure, but his insides shake.

"Yes, sire," Sir Maurius says. "We are prepared. I will alert the king's guard."

"It might begin with the people," King Owen says.

Sir Maurius looks at his king, and his gaze is unwavering. "I will counsel the men," he says.

King Owen feels simultaneously relieved and sorrowful. He clears his throat. If someone could convince him that there were good people in this village, he would not wage a war. So he says, "Find the ones who are protecting the children. Bring them here."

"Yes, sire," Sir Maurius says, and he is about to turn again when King Owen speaks in a voice so soft one could ignore it.

He says, "Do you think there are good people here?"

Sir Maurius hesitates, perhaps trying to decide whether the king was speaking to him or ruminating out loud. At last he says, "There are good people everywhere, sire." His eyes shine. "Good is in all of us. It is the world that covers it up."

King Owen shakes his head. "Someone took my daughter."

The words hang between the two men, the two who have known each other since before they could speak, the two who have pledged their lives to nobility—one to a throne and one to a king.

Sir Maurius says, "Evil is not born, sire. It is made." And then, so softly King Owen, this time, could ignore it:

"We all deserve a second chance, do we not?"

He leaves his king with those words.

And the words are large and heavy and important.

King Owen moves to a window and stares out upon the village.

Evil is not born. It is made.

What has made the people in his village evil?

No, not all of them; a few of them. Perhaps more than a few—but still, there are those who have not yet been tainted by greed and gain.

His thoughts turn back to his mother. She believed a dark magic was slowly creeping across the land, seeping into the people's hearts. She believed it made them become what they were not born to become.

Evil is not born. It is made.

Does the dark magic exist? Has it found them? And how does one hold onto a heart in the presence of dark magic?

King Owen shakes his head. His mother died talking about this dark magic. Everyone in the castle—his father, even—believed her mind had left her.

But what if she was right?

The king's page enters with parchment and a quill pen. King Owen thanks him and moves swiftly toward his writing table in the corner of the throne room. It is only minutes before he is finished with his letter. He seals it with a green dragon. He stares at the wax dragon for a moment. He has never understood this seal, but he has used it all his life, as his father did before him, and his grandfather and all the ancestors before, all the way back to Dale Enderling, the founder of all these lands.

Dale Enderling, who ceded the most powerful land for the tropical one.

King Owen shakes his head. He wonders what Grandfather Dale would think about the king of Fairendale now—a descendant of the kingdom of Lincastle.

What if it had been King Owen?

But it could not have been; King Owen does not possess the gift of magic (gift or curse? It has never been officially decided in the kingdom of Lincastle.).

King Owen lets out a long breath. His page says, "Would you like me to send the letter, sire?" King Owen shakes his head.

"I must talk with my people first," he says. "Prepare them for what may be coming."

"And what is that, sire?"

King Owen looks at his page. He is a small boy, only a few years older than his daughter. King Owen's mouth goes dry, and his heart twists. He shakes his head, trying to get his bearings. "It very well could be a war." He looks back at the parchment. He thinks about the words he has written: *The kingdom of Lincastle will not follow the command of King Willis of Fairendale. We will keep our children safe. We will defend this land if anyone comes for them.*

Sometimes war is inevitable. Sometimes sacrifice is necessary for the greater good.

King Owen tucks the letter into a pocket of his black cloak and lifts his eyes to his page. "Tell Sir Maurius to call a meeting, in the village square." King Owen lifts his chin. "It is time I address my people."

Mira has been dreading this moment all morning.

She must tell Calvin she has been Summoned.

She must tell him everything.

Earlier this morning, before the sun even rose in the sky, Mira (who is known as Cook in the castle of Fairendale) had almost finished her Protection spell over Fairendale castle—a spell that keeps monsters out, though one has breached its invisible wall—when she heard the summoning music.

Mira—Cook—is a shape shifter. Someone has summoned her for a mission. She assumes it is the three

Graces, who are the only ones who have this power over shape shifters. The Graces are watchers of the realm, protectors of the seven kingdoms, and though they cannot change the future, they can influence it. Mira does not know what she has been called to do, but she knows she must answer the call.

She has been delaying her departure.

For the boy.

Calvin has worked with Mira in the castle kitchen since he was a young boy. He was orphaned by a Fire Mountain in the land of Ashvale and happened to be visiting his aunt and uncle in Fairendale when his family perished—an aunt and uncle who did not want to keep him. Mira found a place for him here.

Over the years she has grown fond of the boy. She knows he, too, has grown fond of her.

That is why the leaving will be so difficult. Mira has only just returned from another mission—to collect and secure a strange magical spinning wheel, which she and her fellow shape shifters buried beneath the Great Tree of Helomoth inside the woods near Rosehaven, which are known as the Whispering Woods.

She hopes what she must do this time does not involve a magical spinning wheel; her memories are still fresh and full of the pain and burning that accompanied touching that wheel. Powerful magic ran through the wood. Dark magic. She never wants to touch it again.

Mira lets out a long breath and looks around the garden. She has bolstered it with an extra Abundance spell. She hopes the boy will understand why she must leave so soon after she has returned, though she does not expect him to. He is only a boy, hardly a man. And a leaving so close to the last one would be hard for anyone to understand.

She dislikes leaving him in charge of so much. The servants at Fairendale castle left long ago, leaving not a trace. Only Mira and Calvin and the king's page, Garth, remain.

At least Calvin will have a friend when Mira is gone.

Calvin is in the kitchen, as he always is of late. It is as though he does not want to let Mira out of his sight. Even now, he is looking nonchalantly through the window that faces the gardens, tracking her every move.

Mira swallows hard. He will be fine. He will.

She will show him what to do, and he will keep the castle protected, even if he has no magic. She will collect some. She will give him the stone. He will use it.

He will be fine.

Mira opens the door and steps into the kitchen. Calvin glances at her and continues cutting vegetables.

She says, "Calvin." Her voice is low and soft.

He sets down the knife but does not turn. She waits for him to look at her, and, at last, he does. His eyes shine.

So he already knows.

"Calvin," she says again, softer this time.

He shakes his head, and the tears begin to stream down his face. They draw tears from her eyes as well.

Many recent nights, as she labored to prepare the next day's meals, Calvin fell asleep in a wooden chair. He let her out of his sight, but only because of exhaustion. She carried him to bed, tucked him in, even kissed his forehead.

She presses her hand against the ache in her chest.

"I must go somewhere," she says at last.

Calvin casts his gaze to the floor. "I know."

"How do you know?" Mira says.

Calvin shrugs. "I can feel it." He rubs his chest, too. "In here."

He lifts his eyes to her then, and she sees something, something that alarms her. She says, "What is it?"

He says, "The monster came in here." His voice shakes.

Mira takes two steps into the kitchen and stops. "Why?" she says.

"She was…looking for something." Calvin wrings his hands together. "She said she could smell it. Magic."

Mira feels a jolt in her chest. Heat climbs up her neck.

Calvin says, "I did not tell her anything."

Mira nods. "Just so," she says.

"Do you think she will come back?"

Mira would like to tell him that Yasmin, the monster, will not return to the kitchen. But after she gives him the stone, will Yasmin be able to smell that, too? Such a concentration of magic is desirable for one who does not possess the gift.

She wonders, briefly, if giving Calvin the stone will make more trouble for him. But it will protect him. It will link him to her, so long as he keeps it. He will simply have to be careful.

The silence between them is thick and heavy, until Calvin says, "Why must you leave?"

Mira hears what he does not say: *Why must you leave me?*

Before she can answer, Calvin continues. "You only just got back."

Mira nods. "I know," she says. Her eyes burn. "But I have been Summoned."

"Summoned?" Calvin says. "What does that mean?"

"I have been called to go elsewhere," Mira says.

"Yes, but where? And why? And when will you return?"

Mira shakes her head. She does not tell him that she does not know if she will return. She only says, "I do not know yet."

"Then how do you know you must go?" Calvin looks at her as though he does not believe her.

Mira says, "I have heard the Summoning Song."

Calvin looks more confused than ever. Mira takes a deep breath and begins her explanation with, "I am different than you are."

"Yes," Calvin says. "You are a sorceress."

Mira holds her finger to her lips, quieting him. She glances toward the door that leads out into the castle hallway. Then she says, "I am also something more."

Calvin's eyes are wide. "I know what you are. You are a shape shifter. I have seen you as a bear."

"Have you?" Mira says. But she is not altogether surprised. She tilts her head and studies the boy.

"When King Willis sent you to find the invisible house. And the woman who could help King Willis capture the lost children. The Enchantress." Calvin looks at her, his eyes troubled. And she knows there is something more she must say.

She stares at the ground when she says, "If I had found the lost children, I would have let them go."

Calvin does not speak for a long time. At last, he says, "I would have done the same."

Mira smiles at him. He smiles back, but it wavers at the corners.

She crosses the room with a long stride—she is a tall woman. Calvin backs against a wall, his eyes growing wider, as though he is afraid of her, as though he does not want her to move any closer, as though she is a monster like the one who sits on Fairendale's throne. Mira's chest nearly burns itself up.

She slides a bit to the left, pretending that she was not coming for him, was not moving to take him in her arms, was not feeling motherly at all. It is better this way. She reaches beneath a table and takes out what she planned to give him. She holds the smooth white stone in her hand for a minute, two, three, as she channels magic inside it. On one side is a green patch. It begins to glow.

It takes all her strength to turn around and face the boy, to hand him the stone, to say, in a wispy voice, "I want you to have this," before she is falling toward darkness.

"Cook!" Calvin says, and then his arms are around her, guiding her gently to the stone floor. "What is wrong?"

She does not answer but says, "You must hide this stone. It is full of magic. Magic you can use to keep the gardens producing food, to prepare meals, to protect the castle." She looks at him and rests a palm against his cheek. His eyes are so sad she nearly kisses his forehead. "Magic that can Summon me."

It was once said, much earlier in our story (book number five, to be exact), that Cook was not an eloquent speaker. You must understand that this was merely a part she played—that of an innocent cook. Mira is, in fact, well versed and well read, a highly intelligent woman.

And she is done with playing a part.

Calvin looks down at his right palm, where the small stone sits. His left arm is around Mira's back, propping her up. Calvin's umber eyes burn her face. "You will come when I call? You would do that for me?"

Mira swallows the words she would like to say (which are, "I would do anything for you, Calvin"), and says, instead, "Do not use it lightly. Only if you really need it."

"And you will come?"

"If I am permitted," Mira says. "My first responsibility is to the task before me, whatever it may be. But I will come as soon as I am able."

Calvin stares at the stone, his thick brown eyebrows

becoming slashes that rise toward the middle of his forehead. "But—"

"Listen," Mira says, her voice still papery thin. "This stone can only be used three times between sunup and sundown."

Calvin nods.

"One of those uses must be for castle protection," Mira says. "Press the stone against the castle wall, say the word 'protect,' and it will do its work." Her voice rasps out the last bit: "Use it wisely."

Calvin shakes his head this time. "I do not think I can manage without you," he says. His voice is so small Mira would like to wrap her arms around him and remain here forever.

But she knows she cannot. So she says, "You are brave and strong and kind. You can do anything, Calvin."

"But Cook—"

"My name is Mira," she says, and then she adds her other two names, the ones few people know. She nods toward the stone. "And when you need me, all you have to do is call me by name."

"Take me with you," Calvin says.

How she wishes she could. "I am going where you cannot go," Mira says. "You are not a shape shifter."

"Then make me one," Calvin says.

Mira shakes her head. "It does not work that way, Calvin. I am sorry."

She is sorry for so much.

"Please," Calvin whispers. "Do not leave me."

Mira straightens herself, a pain shooting through her side. She struggles to her feet, Calvin helping her. She looks at the boy for a moment before taking his hand and curling his fingers around the white stone. "I am right here," she says. She places the flat of her hand against his chest. "And here as well."

The tears run down Calvin's face, but he says no more.

Mira looks at him for a long time, memorizing his face, his tears, the love showing plainly in his eyes. She lets herself feel the fierce, protective, motherly love that pulses through her.

And then she turns away.

She does not look back. If she looks back, she will stay. And the world will be all the worse for it.

When Mira reaches the Weeping Woods, she trades her human skin for bear skin, but no shifting will dampen the fire of human love.

She will make it back to Calvin. She will.

She must.

Calvin stares out the window, toward the Weeping Woods where Cook—Mira—disappeared. He stares for a very long time.

Then he drops his eyes to the white stone in his hand. It is cold and smooth and unlike anything he has ever seen before. The green patch on its bottom—or top?—shimmers, and it is as though it contains all the shades of green in one lovely piece. There is the green of the forest; the green of his mother's eyes, which he still remembers; the green of life.

What can go wrong with this stone—this piece of life—in his possession?

He presses the stone into his palm, closes his eyes, and slides it into a pocket of his breeches.

He will carry on. He will do what must be done. Mira believes he can do it; he will believe her.

The stone feels warm against his hip. He stifles the urge to take it out again. The monster came looking for magic. The monster must not know about *this* magic.

Calvin closes his eyes one more time, to call up the face of Mira. He saw the way her face faded into one that was young and lovely when she told him her name.

Perhaps she has worn a mask all this time, to avoid being seen. But he saw her for a moment. He saw her youth, her vigor, her love.

Love? What does a boy like Calvin know of love? She has left him, has she not? Just like his first mother did. And his father. And the aunt and uncle who could have kept him.

Everyone leaves him, in the end. Why would Mira be any different?

But the stone. It must mean something. He can Summon her anytime he likes. He will not, of course, but he could. It is a promise. A connection. A gift.

So he will do his part. And if the stone means nothing, well, he will still have done his part. And that is all anyone can ask, really.

Freedom

Marion had done well on her own.

Bregdon had worried, when first he had brought this powerful sorceress back to life, with the help of both a djinn and a mermaid to whom Bredgon owed much, and she had refused to join Matilda, or Good Cheer, the first of the Graces, saying she preferred to work alone. Was it good for anyone to work alone? Did not a heart need company?

But Bregdon watched her make the magic mirror, watched her look in on her family, watched her do what was necessary. He saw her place the prophet Folen in the mirror and thought, to himself, that it served Folen right; he was a pompous prophet. Bregdon had never much liked him.

But that was his human side, not his spiritual side,

talking. He worried that Folen would find a way to carry out his purposes—which Bregdon could not guess entirely—from inside the mirror, but it seemed that Marion had done what was best for everyone. Iddo could now live his scientific life freely, without the contempt of his father, and Lincastle was safe from the selfish proclamations of a false prophet.

Still, there was the mystery of Folen's staff. What were all the notches? Bregdon longed to ask Marion, but she preferred to work alone, so he left her well enough alone.

For now. There would come a time when he would guide her in her use of the magic mirror, when he would whisper something in her mind, when he would not show up but would be right beside her.

Bregdon knew how to accomplish such things; he had lived many lives.

He could not say why he had lived many lives; he simply had. It was as though he were a man who could never die. He was not a prophet bound to his one hundred forty-third year for his One Last Great Act (which is a prophet's one last chance to use the magic they once had to bring about a crucial change in the trajectory of the world); he was able to execute his One Last Great Act anytime he wished. Either that or he had lived, so far, five one hundred forty-third years.

Each time he executed his One Last Great Act, he died. And rose again.

He did not question it for now. Magic, he knew, did not always make sense. It did not always play by its own rules. He did what was required, and he helped the realm. He did.

He gazed into his looking ball and watched Marion. He watched her turn away from the domestic scene flickering in her mirror. He watched her wipe away a tear and straighten her back. He watched her make the mirror go dark.

Yes. He had helped the realm.

Bregdon came upon knowledge in the same way he came upon life: mysteriously. He had ways of knowing things that no other prophet had. Sometimes the knowledge of the world—the knowledge of the future—simply came to him, as though he had always known it. He had never been wrong. It was unusual for a prophet to have the success rate he did. Bregdon did not question from where the knowledge came, as he did not question from where the multiple chances at life came; he simply took it in grateful hands and did with it what anyone would do: he used it for the greatest good.

Well, perhaps not everyone would use it for the greatest good; he had seen many who had not, it was true. But perhaps that was also a reason Bregdon had been given so many lives to live.

He did not want to seem too self-righteous, but what other reason was there? He could be trusted; he knew this about himself, and it seemed the guiding power of the universe knew it, too.

Well, he could be trusted until now. Bregdon swallowed hard.

He turned the bronze talisman over in his hands. It was the home of the djinn, though a more recent one than others the djinn had occupied in the years of his captivity; djinn were occasionally moved by their masters, from object to object, for purposes unknown—perhaps safety or secrecy or other, more selfish reasons. Some inhabited lamps, some furniture, some jewelry.

The talisman opened like a locket, and when the clasp was pressed, the djinn would burst out on a cloud of blue. Bregdon hesitated. He was ashamed of what he must do, but it was necessary. He had already lost one Grace, since Marion refused to join the future circle of three; he needed the remaining wish, with which he had originally promised to gift Kadesh with his everlasting freedom. But the wish would secure at least a second Grace. A circle of three is best, but a circle of two is better than one.

He would figure out how to bring the third and final Grace into being.

Bregdon took a deep breath and let it out slowly. He traced his finger over the talisman's front, which bore the engraving of a blackbird sitting regally on a blooming branch. It was the symbol of life. It was fitting for a djinn to inhabit such a thing.

With a single pass of Bregdon's hand, the blue cloud billowed from the talisman. Kadesh hovered in the air. Bregdon looked at him with mournful eyes. Kadesh looked back, and his face crumpled for a moment, but he quickly wiped away his disappointment with a brush of his hand. "Your wish is my command," he said in a strong and booming voice. The trees shook. Bregdon closed his eyes and opened them again. He hated what he had to do, but he would promise the djinn his freedom, and he knew how he would do it.

Bregdon said, "I have need of my last wish."

Kadesh said nothing, but his face said everything. *You are just like all the others,* it said. *A selfish, self-serving man.*

Bregdon wanted to protest, but he knew it was halfway true. He was using the last wish for something other than what he had promised the great djinn. And after all the djinn had done for him—had done for the realm.

His heart ached as he said, "The realm needs another Grace."

Kadesh lifted his chin. "Your wish is my command," he said again. There was no personal note of familiarity, no acknowledgment of the history that Bredgon and Kadesh had shared these last several decades. Bregdon felt the sting of this barb.

"Where is she?" Kadesh said.

"She will be dying any minute now," Bregdon said.

Kadesh nodded and turned away.

"Kadesh," Bregdon said.

"Do not speak to me as if you know me, Old Man," Kadesh said.

Bregdon rubbed his throbbing chest. "Kadesh," he said again, but the djinn kept his back turned toward him. So he continued, without the strange orange eyes of the djinn fastened on him. "I have a plan. A plan to free you."

The djinn whirled around. "There is no plan that will work except the giving of a wish," Kadesh hissed.

Bregdon shook his head. "No. I know another way."

The djinn crossed his arms and looked down his nose. "What other way is possible?" he said.

Bregdon dropped his eyes to the ground and raised them back to the djinn. "I will use my One Last Great

Act."

The djinn's face softened. Everyone in the realm—even a djinn trapped in an artifact—knew about a prophet's One Last Great Act. It was an act of sacrifice, an act that would demand a prophet's life.

And though Bregdon might return to life, as he had done so many times before, it would not change the sacrifice, would it? He did not mention his life after life; he merely nodded at the djinn. "You deserve your freedom. After all you have done."

Kadesh drew closer to him. Djinn always carried with them a breath of icy cold, and it hit Bregdon in the chest, but he did not shiver. He would not. The djinn deserved to be treated as a human. In a world where djinn were only valued as much as they could grant wishes, Bregdon knew it was unusual for them to be regarded as someone worthy of dignity and honor. But it was no less than Bregdon himself would wish to be regarded.

Looking at people—however magical, however blue, however kind or cruel—as animals, as less than human beings, as something to be used for gain and nothing else, was a slippery slope into becoming less than human yourself.

Bregdon had always tried to look upon all as equals, djinn included.

Kadesh was right by his side now. He said, "You would do that for me?"

"It is no less than I would want someone else to do for me," Bregdon said.

"But—"

"I am prepared to die," Bregdon said. "You are worth the sacrifice."

He could see the effect the words had on the djinn. A warmth spread over his skin. The djinn smiled, and it was as though a sun beamed from his eyes.

"I only ask that you grant this last wish, and then I will give you your freedom," Bregdon said.

Kadesh nodded. "Yes. Of course I will do it."

"For the good of the realm."

"For the good of the realm." The djinn lifted his hand, and Bregdon pressed his palm against the djinn's. It was the djinn way of saying many things—I am sorry for doubting you, I am grateful to you, I understand you. Bregdon thought this particular gesture meant them all.

The world tilted, and Bregdon could see the woman, could see the light shining around her, could see the flapping robe of the Grim Reaper. He shouted, but he could not see Kadesh. He feared for a moment that all would be lost, that the Grim Reaper would get the woman, a queen named Vivian. If they lost her…

But they did not. Bregdon could hear Kadesh's roar, though he could not see him. A blue cloud swept toward Queen Vivian and enveloped her. The world shook for minutes, hours, days, perhaps. And when it was done, the woman lay on the ground of the forest, the Grim Reaper nowhere near her. She blinked at Bregdon and Kadesh and tried to raise herself up on her elbows.

"Please," Bregdon said, "Lie back down. Good Cheer will be here soon. I will remain with you until she arrives."

When the woman closed her eyes again, Bregdon nodded at Kadesh. "I promise I will free you."

Kadesh stared at him for a moment, and then, with another puff of blue smoke, he was gone. Bregdon stared at the talisman and tucked it back beneath the collar of his robe. In moments Good Cheer arrived.

When Bregdon was finished with all he needed to do —the introductions, the explanations, the half-hearted refusals—he returned to the forest, where he again summoned the djinn.

They stood looking at one another. "Thank you," Kadesh said. "For your sacrifice."

"Thank you for your service, Kadesh," Bregdon said. "Perhaps we shall meet again."

"I hope it is so," Kadesh said.

Bregdon said the words of the ancient Freedom spell, which was generally used for those who were imprisoned in dungeons. Bregdon assumed it would work on a djinn, who was imprisoned in a different way. He finished the spell with, "You are your own master now. Use your freedom well." He was permitted enough time to see the legs form on Kadesh, powerful muscles that ended in rather large blue feet. He saw the smile shine from the former djinn's face. He saw the golden bracelets wrapped around Kadesh's wrists snap and disintegrate.

He heard the words, "It worked."

And then Bregdon fell to the earth, a crumpled mass of skin and bone and muscle and tissue and magic. Kadesh bent to pick up the Old Man's form from the forest floor and carried him to a spot just inside the village of Lincastle, where he might be found by those passing by.

Kadesh walked toward the trees, and he did not turn back.

If he had turned back, he might have seen the prophet's body disappear behind a smoky green haze. He might have seen a collection of silver sparkles crackle through the air. He might have seen a man righted back on his feet, ready to do what must be done next.

Bregdon lived another life.

Across the miles, in the village of Fairendale, a talisman appeared inside Fairendale castle, dangling from a hook in the bedchambers of the king. It replaced the imitation one given to King Sebastien by his father on his sixteenth birthday. (Sebastien's father had not known it was an imitation; he had secured it from the prophet Iddo, who also had not known that the talisman he created had been stolen from where he buried it. But that story will be told soon enough.)

Though it no longer contained a djinn, this talisman contained magical power, and it could be felt by any who touched it. It held the magical power of life. Protection. Fortification.

All born in greater supply, from freedom.

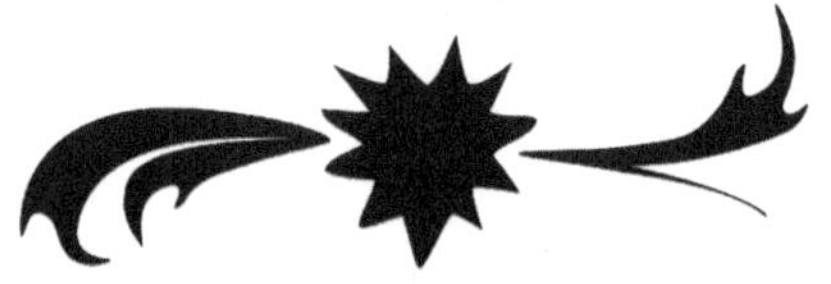

Visions

The same day Frederick hatched from a spider egg sack, several hours after he is beginning to (frightfully, perhaps) adjust more to life as a spider, Sparso announces that it is time for a spider hunt.

Frederick thinks he and the other hatchlings will remain in the nest while the others hunt, but Demarek, her voice bordering urgent, says, "Are you coming, Frederick?"

No, he would like to say. No, the last thing he wants to do is figure out what these spiders hunt. He has been out once now already—not for a hunt but for acclimating himself to the new world, Demarek said—and he has seen what kind of spiders they are.

Giant spiders. Larger than grown men.

What if he has to hunt people?

He cannot do it.

Perhaps Demarek senses his hesitation; she says, "All hatchlings must accompany the spiders for the first hunt."

"But I do not want to go alone," Frederick says. He is aware of Sparso's eyes watching him. Always watching him. He has been alive only a few hours, and he is already weary of the watching.

How could magic expect him to be both a boy and a spider? Why was he brought here to this land? Of everything he could possibly be, why is he a spider?

Demarek nudges Frederick forward. "You must accompany them into the woods." She leans closer, all eight of her eyes focused on him. "You must at least try."

"But—"

"If you want to live," she says, and that is all.

Frederick understands that his life is in danger; it is simply that he does not want to go.

"What do they hunt?" he says. His voice quakes in the asking.

Demarek does not answer his question. All she says is, "Try your best." This time all eight of her eyes are focused on Sparso.

Frederick, too, looks at the spider. He is so much larger than any spider Frederick ever encountered in his life as a boy. How did he not know about these spiders?

How had they remained hidden, beasts as enormous as these? Is this what his mother and father were talking about when they warned Frederick and his sister to stay out of the woods?

Frederick shudders. He is glad, for once, that he listened.

"Go on," Demarek says.

And Frederick, because he has no other viable option, follows the spider pack through the caves and out the hole in the rock from which he has only emerged once since he became a spider. The first time he emerged, by Demarek's side, he was shocked into silence. Demarek was as tall as some of the trees in the forest. He thought that perhaps the trees in this forest were smaller than those in Fairendale's Weeping Woods. The first question he asked was "Where are we?" (The Wishing Woods outside of Lincastle.) The second question he asked was, "Who are you?" (He hoped to catch her off guard, but she said the same thing she had already told him: his sister, Princess Demarek of Cerata.)

So Frederick has already processed, mostly, this shock. When he emerges into the trees this time, the sun is no longer around, but he can see just fine. He is not surprised to note that Sparso is even larger than Demarek.

He is glad he did not know about these spiders. He is even gladder that he never met one. He might have died right on the spot, from heart failure.

His mind is consumed with one question: What do they hunt?

Please, his mind says. *Please do not let it be people.*

He will not be able to hunt people. He hopes he never will be able to hunt people.

Frederick thinks of his king. King Willis hunted people. It is why Frederick is here, why he is separated from his family, why he is a spider. King Willis deserves to be hunted.

But no. Frederick knows better. He was taught better. Evil is not born, it is made. They are the words of Frederick's mother, and he hears them as though she has spoken, as though she is here. He looks around, but, of course, she is not. Still, the memory warms him.

Evil is not born, it is made.

That does not erase the anger Frederick feels toward King Willis. He imagines his mother saying, "It should not. Anger at injustice is noble."

What would his mother say to him now? She hated spiders, and how much more would she hate the kind that were larger than her? Would she run from him if he showed up at her door, now?

Frederick's eyes—all eight of them—burn. But he does not have much time to think about any of these things; Sparso says, "Now, little ones. Go find your food."

The spiders begin to move around him, a horrifying wave of snapping and clicking and the rustling of leaves beneath their—feet? He glances down. His legs taper into something, but can it be called feet? He was never much good at science; what did a boy of Fairendale need to know about science, when he was more interested in the art of cooking?

Frederick is the only spider who does not move. Sparso stares at him. Frederick realizes he missed his chance to slip away unnoticed. Will there be another?

He hopes so. Desperately.

"Well?" Sparso says.

Frederick does not know what to say; no question has technically been asked. But he thinks he knows what he must do. He scuttles toward the trees, where perhaps he can hide for a time. He does not know what he is supposed to be hunting, so he will watch.

Sparso remains where he is. After a time, a tiny spider—still large by human measurements, but not compared to the rest of this pack, drops a bird at the feet of Sparso.

"Well done, little one," Sparso says. "You may eat."

The spider does. Frederick turns away.

But at least a bird is better than a human.

He watches three more spiders drop their prey. Another bird, a squirrel, and a porcupine. Impressive. Even Frederick nods when Sparso says, "Very well done."

Frederick turns, and, by a strange stroke of luck, there is a panther. Dead, on the floor of the forest. He stares at it for a moment and then he feels something near him. He turns. It is Sparso. "Well," Sparso says. He walks around the panther, his body impossibly large compared to such a majestic beast. "I believe this one wins them all." Sparso looks at Frederick. "You will dine with me tonight." He begins to drag the beast toward the rock that marks the entrance to the Cave of Cerata. Frederick does not help in the slightest. He feels sick to his stomach.

He did not want to win anything. He does not want to dine with the spider.

But when he returns to the nest and tells Demarek what has happened, she says, "You cannot refuse. It is an honor."

And how to tell Demarek that he is not a spider, he is a boy? He cannot eat a panther. He cannot eat anything that these spiders are eating. What if eating like spiders makes him more of a spider? What if he loses his memories? What if he forgets that he was a boy once upon a time?

Demarek lowers her voice. "Sparso does not hesitate to devour those who are different."

Frederick hears the warning in her voice. But what can he do? He *is* different. How does one pretend otherwise?

Sparso stands in the middle of the throng of spiders —so many! And so large!—and tells of their hunt. He tells of the hatchling who brought the biggest prize: a panther. The spiders murmur. And Sparso says, "Come forward, hatchling. You get the first bite."

Demarek nudges Frederick forward, and he walks on awkward, wooden legs—eight of them!—toward the carcass in the middle of the cave. His stomach turns.

He tries to find a way to avoid eating anything at all. But they are all watching. They are all waiting.

"You do not like this food we have?" Sparso says. All eight eyes flash at Frederick.

"I have only just been born," Frederick says in a very small voice. He knows it is not enough.

"And you do not know how to eat," Sparso says. He takes the panther's head in his mouth and chomps it off with one bite. "This is how," he says, bits and pieces stuck to his chin—that is, if spiders have chins. He certainly has a face, but Frederick cannot tell about chins. For some reason, the faces of the spiders look almost human, but he knows that cannot be so. Spiders could never be humans, could never share anything with humans.

Unless these spiders are an entirely different kind. A human-like beast of the forest. One of those his mother told him about. He does not remember spiders, however. Perhaps no one knew of creatures such as these.

He will tell the stories himself, if he escapes from this awful skin.

When he escapes. He cannot give up hope.

"Eat," Sparso says. It is not loud, it is not angry, it is not threatening. And somehow that makes it worse.

Frederick closes his eyes and nibbles on the side of a leg. He does not like the taste, but he pretends as well as he can. Sparso watches him. Frederick moves to another leg, then the torso, and still the spider watches.

Frederick's stomach will not hold up.

At last, Sparso says, "Enough. Leave some for the other spiders. You cannot eat it all." And Frederick is glad that he has been dismissed and can disappear into the crowd. He feels Sparso's eyes on him as he scuttles away.

He must keep his head down, try not to attract attention. But he fears it is already too late for that. Sparso may never stop watching now. Perhaps he senses that there is something different about Frederick, something off.

Frederick empties his stomach as quietly as he can in one of the cave's passages. Even in the village of Fairendale, even as a boy, he did not eat meat. He did not like the way animals were slaughtered, though the butcher of Fairendale did it in a humane way. He still did not like taking the life of another sacred being. He tended the garden he planted behind his cottage and tried to help with the community gardens of Fairendale, and he prepared for his household food that did not require meat. Even his father, who had been a meat lover before his son turned him around, said that Frederick had a gift with food.

Frederick's whole body aches. How he wishes he could go home.

"You did well, little one," Demarek says.

"My name is Frederick," Frederick says.

Demarek turns her eyes on him, and the two in the front are piercing blue again, for only a moment. "Frederick?" she says. "You must not tell anyone that. You will be given a name on the Naming Day. You do not have a name yet."

"But I do," Frederick says.

Demarek lets out a breath and closes her very human eyes. When they open again, they are black beads. But

Frederick knows he did not imagine it. "You will not last long in this pack, Frederick, if you do not follow rules."

Frederick wonders if he was wrong to trust Demarek with his words, with his name, with the knowledge that he is something other than a spider. Do spiders understand these nuances? Do they draw conclusions? Do they intuit magic?

But Demarek is not like the others, either.

Frederick knows he should not ask, but he does so anyway. "What would happen to me? If I do not follow the rules?"

Demarek is silent for a moment before she says, "Spiders who do not conform and stay with the pack and do what is expected of them are imprisoned." He can tell she is not finished. She continues. "Spiders who are imprisoned are eaten when food grows scarce." She does not look at him when she says, "We do not think twice about eating our own kind."

Frederick's stomach gives another heave, but he manages to swallow his sickness down. He says, "You eat your own kind?"

"Of course," Demarek says. "It is the way of spiders like us."

"And what kind of spiders are you?" Frederick says, not even realizing he has excluded himself from them.

"We—and you—are Gulonon spiders."

"I have never heard of them."

"We hide out well." Demarek gestures with two hands —hands? Legs? Feet?—toward the cave's walls. "We remain underground and out of sight."

"And you are the only ones?" Frederick says.

"Oh, no," Demarek says. "Sparso has a brother with his own family. He lives near Fairendale." She turns all her eyes on Frederick, as though she knows.

He tries his best not to react to this news, but inside his heart is saying *Fairendale. Fairendale. Fairendale.*

Another thought trails it: *That is where I will go.*

And for the first time since becoming an enormous spider, Frederick feels a small spot of hope bloom in him.

In the dragon land of Eyre, slightly east of Rosehaven, a group of dragons gathers in a large cave. Appearing in various shapes and sizes (the dragons of Eyre are able to shift themselves into different sizes and shapes, some of them appearing as salamanders, some of them as tiny green bees), they huddle around their dragon king, Rezedron, who is dying of a wound he sustained from the thorn of one of Rosehaven's poisonous white roses.

He believes it is a curse. Dark magic running through his veins, destroying his body from the inside out.

The dragons have gathered to hear what they might be able to do for their king; they do not want Rezedron to die. They are willing to do practically anything.

Their reasons are complicated, as are most all reasons. Of course they love their king; he has been a good king in the years he has led them. But they also fear for their future.

When a dragon king dies in the land of Eyre, the son of the dragon king inherits the throne. But Rezedron never had a son, only a daughter, Nischal, and the old laws (which Rezedron, and many more than he would suspect, believes are outdated and in need of revising) say a female cannot rule the dragon throne of Eyre.

In the case of no heir, the crown is passed to the fastest and strongest of the dragons, determined by a contest. In this case, that would be the dragon Vyrmoss, who is not here and who would be furious to know that the dragons called a meeting to which he was not invited.

No one wants to see Vyrmoss rule the throne, even if he *is* the fastest and strongest dragon among them. He is also the cruelest, the one most obsessed with power, the most reckless. And this, most of the dragons believe, is a recipe for disaster. They care about their land. They care about their current king. And so here they are.

"Well, my friends," Rezedron says. "It has come to my attention that my council would like me to find a cure."

Nischal draws closer to her father. "Not only your council." Her violet eyes move out to the crowd. "Your dragons."

Rezedron nods. He has been unable to move himself from this cave in many, many weeks. He has not seen or addressed his people since his useless legs trapped him here.

It has been nearly a year since he has taken to the sky and felt the freedom of flying. He misses being a dragon. And the end has not been swift. It has been torturously long—so long that he, now, is entertaining his daughter's proposition: search for a cure.

He knows where a cure is.

Rezedron looks around at his dragons. They are small, some of them practically invisible, but he can see all their eyes, of every different shade. They make this cave beautiful. Why did he never think to do this before?

And what if it is too late now?

He shoves the thought away and says, "So I suppose we must search for a cure." He clears the emotion from his throat. "And I must warn you: it will be dangerous."

"We will risk our lives for you," says a dragon near the front. Wirena. His mate's sister. She is smaller than an iguana but larger than a lizard. Rezedron feels massive next to her.

She draws close to him and nearly touches his side when Rezedron roars, "Do not touch me!"

Wirena draws back, her eyes glowing violet, the same shade his mate's used to be. But it is not sorrow that lifts his words and spins them into the air; it is concern. "I do not know if it is contagious."

Wirena looks at him for a moment longer and nods. "We will find your cure," she says. "You will live."

Nischal's eyes fill, and Handriss and Lago, Nichal's best friends, nod. The rest of the dragons blink their agreement. The cave shimmers.

When all has stilled again, Rezedron swallows hard and says, "Why? I am an old dragon. Perhaps it is time for someone younger, someone—"

"We want our king," Lago says. "We want you." Her orange eyes shine.

He nearly asks his question again when Handriss steps forward, her blue eyes slicing into him. "Because you are a good king. Because we deserve a good king. Because your time is not over." She hisses the last part, so others will not hear. "Because you have a daughter who deserves a throne."

Yes. His daughter deserves a throne, and if Rezedron lives long enough, perhaps he can convince the dragons to change the law.

"The cure will not be easy to find or secure," Rezedron says.

"No matter," says Wirena.

"Long live Rezedron," says a dragon from the back, and the dragons lift up the words, a chant, a rallying cry.

Rezedron sighs. Well. He will tell them what he knows. When they have quieted he says, "You will have to fly into the land of the Savage Gardens. There is a creature that guards them. When the creature is slain, a flower grows from its body. The flower is the cure."

"Only one?" Nischal says. Her voice falters slightly, a small hitch that speaks to her uncertainty. "Only one such being exists?"

"I know of only one," Rezedron says. "The flower that grows from its carcass removes curses." He glances down at his rotting legs. "All curses."

He knows his dragons will not like this; they are docile dragons who value all life, unless they are in need of food. Unless they are in need of life sustenance.

Does this count? Is saving a king worth killing

another, perhaps the last of its kind?

Well, they will have to decide how they feel about that. Rezedron has told them what he knows.

The cave is silent for some moments, while the dragons, Rezedron hopes, think about the cost.

"There must be another way," Nischal says.

"I know of no other," Rezedron says. "But perhaps you could find one. You were always good at asking questions." He smiles briefly in her direction. Nischal's eyes are sad. She knows. She knows they cannot do this, cannot violate their morals for a life that will pass eventually.

"How do you know this?" says another dragon, Frinnet. His eyes are a yellow-gold color.

"It is a legend," Rezedron says.

"A legend." A voice bangs into the cave. The other dragons turn. Rezedron does not even need to look. He knows to whom this voice belongs: Vyrmoss.

The young dragon moves into the opening of the cave. He remains his normal, massive size. His red eyes flash. "I see you have called a meeting without me."

Rezedron wonders how many other dragons wait outside, already having chosen Vyrmoss over Rezedron. He never would have thought something like this could happen, but youth is often foolish.

"It was not intentional," Nischal says. Her violet eyes darken and flash.

"Of course not," Vyrmoss says, but his eyes say otherwise. He knows. He does not advance deeper into the cave but remains at the mouth. He says, "How do you know this flower will cure you and will not simply take the life of many of your dragons?" His red eyes glow.

"I do not know for sure," Rezedron says. "But an enchantress, in the very beginning, told me that this was the way." He had remembered it in a dream.

"An enchantress," Vyrmoss says. "You went to an enchantress." He lets the words hang there, lets them sink into the skin of the other dragons. He finishes with: "We do not trust people with magic. We do not trust people at all!" This last part he roars.

Some of the other dragons stir—uncomfortable with this disturbing revelation or uncomfortable with Vyrmoss's show of anger? Rezedron is, after all, still the dragon king of Eyre.

"I trust her," Rezedron says. He gives no explanation why.

After some silence, someone calls out, "Long live Rezedron." Someone else echoes. Vyrmoss's eyes flare, but he says nothing.

"So we will find the cure," Wirena says. "We will bring it back, and we will heal you."

"It may not work," Rezedron says.

"It is worth trying," Lago says.

"The dragon land of Werizod. That is where the creature lives." Rezedron has saved this last bit for an important reason: no one has ever ventured into the dragon land of Werizod. A hush falls over the congregation. Rezedron breaks the silence with, "You do not have to go. This is not an order from your king."

"It is an order," Wirena says. "It is an order to save your life."

Rezedron lifts his head and shakes it vigorously, though it pains him so much he nearly roars. "No," he says. "I cannot ask my people to die for me."

"You do not have to ask," says a dragon in the back, shaped like a chameleon. "It is what we do."

"We will go," says another, who slithers forward as a green snake. One by one the other dragons step forward as well, until only Vyrmoss remains where he is, and any dragons who may already follow him, hidden from sight. When he is the only one standing on the invisible line between who will go find their king's cure and who will not, he spins, his tail slashing at the cave wall, crumbling a bit of it, and lumbers away.

For a fleeting moment, Rezedron wonders if Vyrmoss will try to sabotage the hunt of the other dragons, but he pushes the thought from his mind. There are other important matters. Such as keeping his daughter safe.

Rezedron again addresses the crowd. "You will fly out at first light," he says. "Nischal will remain here, with me."

His daughter's head snaps in his direction, as he knew it would. "What? Father, no."

"Fly safe, and look out for one another. Return to me as soon as you can. Be brave. Be kind. Be strong." The dragons do not move. "Go!" Rezedron roars, and Wirena ushers them from the cave.

Only Nischal remains. She is glowering. "You should have let me go, Father," she says. "No one can track better than I can."

"I know," Rezedron says. "But I needed my heir here."

Nischal meets his eyes. "What?"

"I will change the law, Nischal," he says. "You deserve a throne. If they find a cure—"

"When they find a cure," Nischal says.

Rezedron smiles. "When they find a cure, I will set a new law into motion. A daughter will be a queen."

Nischal's eyes soften, and Rezedron knows she is

pleased.

He falls asleep with this victory on his mind.

King Willis is in the throne room of Fairendale castle, pacing. He paces back and forth and back and forth. When he has paced for the hundredth time or so in front of the mirror, a voice calls out to him.

The king turns, expecting to see his father—dreading it, in fact—but the face that stares back at him is one he does not recall having seen before, one that feels familiar all the same, one he cannot place. The man wears the royal robe of Fairendale, a thick purple one ringed in gold and clasped at its top with a brass bear. But he is fair where King Willis's father, the typical inhabit of the mirror (King Willis did not even know there were other inhabitants!), is dark—golden hair, pale blue eyes, pink cheeks. He looks a good deal kinder than King Sebastien ever did.

Who is this in the mirror, and where is King Sebastien? King Willis shakes his head and closes his eyes.

When he opens his eyes again, the man is still there. And this time his voice is frantic. "Help," he says. "You must help us. There must be some way to let us all out."

Let them all out? Why would he do a thing like that, when his father is trapped inside the mirror? And how? And why? And what if?

King Willis stares at the mirror, his mouth opening of its own accord, his thoughts swirling round and round and round in his mind. He has never seen anyone but King Sebastien in this mirror and now there is—who?

Who is this man?

Who is the "us" to which he refers?

Who is playing tricks on him, using this mirror?

It must be a trick. King Willis closes his eyes again. And this time, when he opens them, the man is gone. The mirror is clear. His own image, which has begun shrinking in girth, stares back at him.

He shakes his head. He must have imagined it. He leans closer to the mirror.

Closer. Closer. And closer still.

His face is nearly pressed up against the glass when the man flashes into visibility again with the frantic, breathless words, "Help us." Something shoves the man into the mirror, and though he hears not a sound, King Willis sees the man's face strike the glass, sees him fall, sees his form splayed out on the invisible ground.

What is happening? King Willis backs away from the

mirror, shakes his head, squeezes his eyes shut. He is going mad. He must be. There is no other explanation for what has just taken place.

"Oh, my," he says to the room, but no one is here.

A voice calls from behind him. "It is time for supper sir." King Willis swings around to meet the eyes of his page. Garth.

He remembers the boy's name, still. King Willis almost smiles, if not for the memory of the image in the mirror.

Garth tilts his head. "Are you all right, Your Majesty? You look as though you have seen…" He does not finish his thought.

King Willis rubs his chest and wipes a sheen of sweat from his forehead. "Yes, very well," he says, without answering the boy's question. He moves toward the door. "And what is for supper this evening?"

"Soup," Garth says.

It is the same every night, but King Willis does not mind. He has always enjoyed a bowl of hearty soup.

"Good," King Willis says. "Good."

He only looks back once, and all he sees is the vague outline of the mirror.

He is glad, for once, that his vision is limited.

King Willis then turns his full attention to the task

before him: dining with the monster-woman, Yasmin. He must keep his wits about him. He must be on guard.

For his kingdom.

King Willis seats himself and waits.

Mira was on her way to Lincastle, where the Summoning Song pointed, when something stopped her. A premonition of some sort. A warning. It was cold, razor sharp, leaden. She turned back toward Fairendale and whispered an apology to the wind, in hopes that it would reach the Graces and speak to her slight delay.

She will be there, but she must see to something first.

And now she stands in the empty throne room of Fairendale castle, in front of a mirror. She has not alerted Calvin to her return; she has never liked goodbyes, and she does not want to repeat the leaving.

Where is the monster? Mira looks behind her at the throne room doors—the front and the back ones. But the monster is nowhere to be seen.

She turns her attention back to the mirror. She sees only herself.

But the premonition. There was something. She knows it. Her animal sense has never led her astray.

And as she stares into the mirror, a flash explodes in her eyes. It is not her vision; it is the inside of the mirror. There is a figure that is not hers, and then there is nothing.

She has left plenty of space between her and the mirror, but now she closes the distance. She squints. The mirror is blank, as though it does not even see her. Mira tilts her head. What strange sorcery is this?

Then the mirror moves, shattering in silence, waves rippling out to the edge. There is the figure again, a man with eyes like her own, but with a stronger jaw and shorter, lighter hair. Mira blinks, peers closer, raises a hand to touch the mirror. The image fades and disappears altogether, and once again the mirror is blank.

"What is this?" Mira says aloud. She takes her hand off the glass; the man reappears.

"Help," the man is saying. "Help us. Please. Help us escape."

The mirror clears, and it is Mira's own image reflected back at her now. She stares for a very long time.

She does not understand what she has seen. The face was like her own, but it was not hers. He spoke. To her.

Mira touches the mirror again, and it ripples, but the man does not return.

Her brother? Could it be? And how?

Mira knows she must leave. She cannot remain here, not when she has been Summoned. She backs away from the mirror, her eyes never leaving it until she is out the throne room doors and in the hall.

Then she turns and flees out of the castle, across the lawn, and into the woods. As soon as she is hidden beneath the cover of trees, she flashes into a bear.

On her way to the Summoning.

On her way to report what she has seen and heard.

On her way to change the world.

The monster and the mirror will have to wait.

Stronger

Bregdon had lost count of his many lives. It did not seem to matter; they were more than nine, perhaps more than ten, perhaps more than a dozen. They kept coming, and he could not determine if he was more glad or more pained by their regularity. He had, after all, lost everyone he loved. He even lost track of Kadesh, not wanting to impinge on the djinn's tentative freedom.

But strange things began to happen. When Visions came upon Bregdon, he found that he was too exhausted to lift himself from wherever he had fallen (and he always fell as soon as the Vision crackled around the edges of his sight). So he would sleep. Sometimes for days. Nothing ever harmed him, as though he had a spell of protection cast over him, but it was impossible to keep track of the hours and days.

He had no need of keeping track, but he still preferred it. Order in chaos; Bregdon had always favored this.

Bredgon walked through forest after forest, on his way to nowhere. He did not know which forest, even, he inhabited; he simply wandered. He was ever on the lookout for the prophet, Rip van Winkle, who had cursed him with this life after life (it is unclear whether Rip, who was Bregdon's rival and jealous of Bregdon's powerful prophetic abilities, actually did curse Bregdon, but the "curse" and Bregdon's magical return from exile were always linked in his mind). Bregdon had once faked death and disappeared—exiled himself far into the uncharted territory of the northern lands—so that he and Rip could coexist. Bregdon, unlike Rip, knew they were both needed. Such were Bregdon's abilities, to see so far into the future that he could forgive Rip for his ignorance. He knew Rip would change the realm in a significant and lasting way.

The problem was that Bregdon's Visions no longer contained Rip. And, too, Bregdon had been brought out of exile, which was not supposed to happen unless Rip died.

Where was the prophet? Bregdon needed to find him, needed to know he was still alive to do what was in his destiny to do.

It had become an obsession, and every time Bregdon lived a new life, he began it with the search.

This particular day, Bregdon was trying to See into the future, but the future would not cooperate. He sat down on a log, to think about all he knew and the future that remained unconfirmed. A prophet can See the future, but they are not assured of that future. Many acts and decisions can alter it, which is why a prophet is always on duty, so to speak.

Just as Bregdon was preparing to rise from this log, a Vision sparkled into his sight.

He saw a home, and he peered, with his prophet eyes, into its windows. Within it was the unfolding of destruction: a small girl with brown hair and eyes of the same, a mother lying on a bed burning from the inside out, a father who forbade magic.

The Grim Reaper was waiting. The Grim Reaper, in fact, had caused this destruction. And it was destruction all over the land of White Wind.

What did he want with this woman? Bregdon watched the Grim Reaper watch her with hungry eyes.

He knew he must do something. And he knew he was not strong enough to do it himself.

Oh, how he hated to do what he must do. But only

djinn and mermaids had the kind of power that could save a life from the Grim Reaper. Rumors added Mages to that list, but Bregdon had never confirmed it. He did not count necromancers; it was not the right kind of magic, since the dead they raised remained dead.

He stared at the ground for some minutes. He considered. He reconsidered. He already owed the mermaid much—too much. And mermaids never forget.

The djinn, however…

Bregdon shook his head. He must do this himself.

But what if he could not? What if he lost this woman so desired by the Grim Reaper that the specter waited outside her house for her spirit to depart? What then? He asked the Vision to show him, but it would not.

It is not widely known in the magical world that a djinn granted freedom can always be Summoned by calling his true name. Some well-read masters use their first wish to command that a djinn reveal his or her true name. A djinn is never happy to do so, and usually, when a master procures the name, a djinn knows he or she will not be granted freedom with a third wish.

Bregdon never asked Kadesh for his true name. He simply knew it.

He had always taken great care with this knowledge.

The life of a djinn is a difficult one. When a djinn is

Summoned out of freedom, he turns into a slave who walks, rather than one who is trapped in a magical object. Neither one, of course, is desirable. Bregdon did not want a slave. But he did not know how to accomplish what he needed done without the powerful magic of a djinn. The magic of a djinn is of a different, stranger, more formidable sort than that of sorcerers. It is more powerful because a djinn is not permitted to use his magic freely; he is permitted to use it only under the direction of a master. It is unknown why this is the way it is, though there is speculation that because a djinn is returned to his magical object, where he sleeps for years —sometimes hundreds of them—he builds up enough strength there to perform amazing feats.

A djinn who has procured his freedom is stripped of his magical abilities, though those abilities are not completely gone but are simply latent. Under the direction of a command and his true name, a free djinn can accomplish magical acts as astounding as one who is bound to a magical object. Some do not enjoy this piece of their freedom; the loss of magic is a difficult sacrifice. Some over the years have begged former masters to put them back in their objects, so their magic will be restored. But most djinn enjoy their freedom and are content with walking through life as a man or a woman, albeit with blue skin.

Bregdon ran a hand through his still-abundant hair and let out a long breath. He would do it. He had to. He could not risk the Grim Reaper capturing the woman and doing who knows what with her.

So he called.

At first it was a whisper. "Kadesh Zuar Eliasaph." Then louder. "Kadesh Zuar Eliasaph." And then Bregdon lifted his face to the sky and shouted, "Kadesh Zuar Eliasaph!"

It always took three.

The djinn appeared before him, as though he had always been walking in the woods. Running, rather. Kadesh was running, a bit of snow on the top of his bare blue head. He stumbled, which slowed him considerably. He looked around, confusion drawing his eyebrows low.

He spotted Bregdon, and that same shining smile broke across his face. "Bregdon," he said. "How did you know I was in need of rescue?"

Bregdon shook his head. He did not know.

The djinn laughed. It was a magical sound that seemed to bounce off the trees and dance around them. Kadesh put his hand over his bare blue chest, flattening his darker blue vest ringed in gold. He sounded…happy.

Bregdon's mouth went dry.

"I was about to be captured into another magical object by a giant in the land of Guardia," Kadesh said.

"What were you doing in the land of Guardia?" Bregdon said. No one went to the land of Guardia; it was the land of giants—frost giants, cave giants, rock giants, every kind of giant you can imagine—and the most dangerous dragons in the realm.

Kadesh shook his head. "It matters not," he said. "I am here. And I am still free." The smile slipped from his face when he looked at Bregdon. His eyes narrowed. "Why am I here?"

Bregdon cast his eyes to the ground. How he hated it. "I have need of a favor."

Kadesh did not say anything for a long time. And when he spoke, his voice was soft, sad. "You would make me a slave again?"

Bregdon shook his head. Oh. How he hated it.

"The Grim Reaper," Bregdon said. His voice broke.

The silence wrapped around them, squeezing Bregdon's throat. At last he looked up at the djinn. "I am sorry," he said. The words came out as a whisper.

The orange eyes of Kadesh flashed.

"You know I would not do it if I had another way."

The orange eyes of Kadesh continued to flash for some moments before they softened. His shoulders slumped. "I know."

They were only words, but they meant the world to Bregdon. He said, "I will find a way to free you completely. You will not even be bound by the speaking of your name."

Kadesh shook his head. "It has never been done."

"Neither has a man lived again after his One Last Great Act."

Kadesh's mouth twisted up into a half-smile. "And yet here you stand."

Bregdon allowed himself to smile as well. "And yet here I stand." He looked at his hands and back at the djinn. "I will grant you your permanent freedom."

"I will become a man, as I once was," Kadesh said.

"Yes," Bregdon said. "As soon as you break the bonds of death once more."

Kadesh nodded. "I will do it." He held out his wrists. Bregdon took the golden bonds, which had fallen at his feet after speaking Kadesh's name for the third and final time, and placed them on Kadesh's wrists. "Your wish is my command," Kadesh said.

A tear leaked out the corner of Bregdon's right eye. He said, "Find the woman. Bring her here."

Kadesh nodded and was gone. Bregdon asked for the Vision, and this time his Sight cooperated. He could see the woman, her skin emitting a red glow, as though fire tore through her. He saw the djinn. He saw the other two Graces, fighting too.

And he joined the fight as well.

It took all four of them to save the woman from the hands of the Grim Reaper. But they did. They completed the circle of Graces. They created the magic of Fate.

And in their completion, in their creation, in their solidarity, they all became stronger than Death.

And this would make all the difference in the world, though they did not yet know it.

Resistance

It is early morning, and Frederick has tried as much as he can to keep himself from slipping outside the spider den to explore. But the lure of exploring is simply too great. He used to be chastised for this weakness, if it can be called a weakness, in the land of Fairendale. He wanted to run and observe and experience; his mother and father wanted him to continue his studies so he did not fall behind the other village children. Excellence was their mandate.

He did not explore the woods near Fairendale, of course; he had heard too many stories about the beasts there. But he did venture into the Sleeping Fields once or twice, where he promptly and predictably fell asleep. His mother was none too happy about that; she was tasked with cooking supper in his absence. Not that it was required that Frederick cook supper in his home, but everyone knew that his mother could burn a pot of water. Supper did not taste good when his mother cooked; everyone was grumpy.

Frederick tries to shove thoughts of his mother and father and the life he had in Fairendale far from his mind.

The spiders, he has learned in his limited time with them (and he hopes his observations are not wrong), sleep during most hours of the day and wake and hunt and revel at night. As far as Frederick can guess, this is because they would like to avoid being seen. Their black bodies blend well with the shadows of the night. Frederick will remember this as he moves about; he will be seen much more easily in the light of morning.

The vision of spiders, Demarek has told him, is also much better at night, though Frederick has found that his vision remains both human and spider. It is as though he can put on spectacles and see as a human, minus the color (except for those strange times with Demarek, which Frederick has, now, attributed to his overactive imagination), and then take them off and see as a spider.

It can be disorienting sometimes, but much better than seeing only as a spider. Spiders do not have good vision.

After the feasting ceremony last night, the hatchlings

were taught how to spin webs. Frederick has chosen this as his plan, if someone should discover him sneaking out; he merely wanted to practice his web spinning. Perhaps from the trees, if they will hold him. He is not nearly as large as the grown spiders; he is about the size of a tall man. Wider, but still not enormous.

Upon escape (metaphorically speaking, of course; Demarek, as though sensing Frederick's developing plan for true and permanent escape, told him last evening that the spiders are merciless to traitors. He is too afraid to attempt a true escape at this time, until he can foolproof his plan.), Frederick does practice web making. He draws in them. He enjoyed drawing as a child, and this is a whole new experience for him. He draws a rose in one. He draws a horse in another. In the last, he draws a cottage that looks like the one he lived in all his life until now.

He turns away from it, all eight eyes blurring.

He will play a game now. He will soar from tree to tree—inconspicuously, of course. The sun is not out today, but still, against a gray sky a spider so large and black will be noticed.

So Frederick tries to remain in the treetops, at the very tips, since most people who travel in woods look down but not up. He sees no people traveling, however.

He sees nothing at all.

Still, he feels a cold and shaking fear that he will be discovered—not by people but by the spiders. He does not know what the spiders will do to him if they discover him. Will they see this, too, as betrayal?

He must not think of that. He is determined to explore, to at least, for once, enjoy the movement of a spider.

He will not be one forever. He hopes.

The web creation ability is particularly amazing. Frederick jumps from tree to tree, securing his body with a good bit of thick white silk shooting from his abdomen.

What would Chester and Charles think of him now?

And just like that Frederick's rhythm falters. He misses the next tree and crashes to the ground. He lifts himself on his feet and glances around. The woods are empty. He climbs up the tree and remains there for a moment, his breath heaving in and out.

Where are Chester and Charles? Where are the other Fairendale children? Have they all returned as monstrous beings? Have some of them been lost?

Nothing is guaranteed with a Vanishing spell.

The anger, the sorrow, the frustration sends Frederick back on his way, swinging through the trees. He stops on the edge of the woods, which look out on a village that is not Fairendale. In this village, even the cottages that surround the castle look like tiny castles. He remembers this land from his studies; it is the only one he remembers: Lincastle.

Frederick remains there, at the top of a tree. He lets the sea breeze dry out his eyes; lets the sun rays, reaching for a moment through puffy gray clouds, burn his spider skin; lets the pain on the inside become the pain on the outside.

He is stuck here. He cannot move through the village; he can only move on the outskirts, clinging to the cover of the trees. He would like nothing more than to walk across that golden beach, feel the sand beneath his feet. He had never been anywhere outside the land of Fairendale. He would like to enjoy this.

But he is a spider.

And a spider is unwelcome.

Another memory wriggles into his mind. His father, tasked with removing the spiders and sacs from the corners of their cottage. His father, screaming—a high-pitched, feral sound—when one of those sacs hatched and hundreds of spiders swarmed out. His father, running as fast as Frederick had ever seen his father run.

He knows what spiders do. They scare people.

So Frederick remains, a black ball huddled at the top

of a tree.

It is a difficult, painful thing to be a fearsome creature and to be aware of it. The loneliness alone can be unbearable.

Frederick watches the sleepy town waken. The people step onto the streets, dressed, it seems, in their best. Smoke rises from the taverns, and the smell of real food —fresh bread and fried eggs and breakfast pies—makes Frederick close his eyes.

The longing, too, can be unbearable.

He almost moves forward—until he remembers, once more, with a flash of spearing sadness, that he is a spider.

He is a spider.

He is a monster.

He is alone.

He would rather be in the dungeons beneath the dungeons of Fairendale castle. Why did he run when the king's men invaded Fairendale? Why did he continue running? At least in the dungeons, he would have company. He would have arms and legs. He would be a human.

He would be trapped. Would it be better?

Yes, he tells himself.

No.

Frederick's mind is a muddle. He turns his attention

back to the streets. He will live vicariously through its people. He will watch them walk, observe them talk, and imagine them eat and drink and be merry.

The people in this village dress like kings and queens—all, that is, except for those who are on the southernmost point of the land, closest to the sea. They are dressed in rags.

Frederick wonders at this. He is, in truth, appalled by it. Rich and poor, so obviously disconnected. He notices a young, bedraggled girl, skipping near the others like her. Her face shines with a joy that Frederick would like to have. And once again, he nearly moves out from the trees, drawn by an invisible hand. He remembers just in time and balls himself back up.

The girl, clad in a faded red dress, skips past everyone, speaking to them, leaning over them, touching their faces. Then she skips toward the sand along the beach.

After a time, the girl disappears from his view. Frederick decides to follow her. He can move along the line of trees, toward the water's edge, but he knows he will not be able to scuttle across the sand without being detected. And detection means fear. He does not want to frighten anyone. He is not so large as Sparso or Demarek, but he is still large. Larger than the girl. What would she think?

He moves carefully, as silently as he can. The limbs bow somewhat when he climbs onto them, but he does not think anyone will notice. The trees bend often in the sea breeze. And here the trees have large pink leaves, so many of them that one cannot see into the branches. They are good hiding places.

The girl is sitting under one of these pink-leafed trees, her back leaning against its trunk. How fortunate. He will be able to hover above her, and she will not be able to see him. He can see her face from where he is. She has small gray eyes and golden hair.

Frederick's aim is perfect. He pulls himself into the tree beneath which is the girl. He wraps himself in silk, so as to appear like a leaf—albeit a very large gray one—if she happens to peer through the branches. Shadows can turn pink to gray, can they not?

He sees now that the girl is not sitting on the ground but is curled into a low wooden seat that is cushioned with a red pillow and looks to have been made quite finely, which is the exact opposite of her clothes. She stirs a silver spoon into a brown bowl of what looks like mush.

Frederick is familiar with mush. It was all he usually had for breakfast, though he tried, endlessly, to spice it up with herbs and fruit to make it more palatable. It was still mush. He sympathizes with the girl, though she does not complain and only halts her song (she has a lovely voice) when she has taken a bite and can no longer fit anything in her mouth.

She takes a bite, chews for a bit, and then she sings.

Frederick closes his eyes. It is good to be so close to a human. It is good to hear a lovely voice singing a lovely song.

Frederick remains as he is, wrapped in silk, dangling from a limb, hidden by flowers, for a long time. He watches the girl eat, and he watches her stare out at the sea, and he watches her smile to herself. He tries to absorb some of her joy. It has been so very long since he has felt the kind of joy that is so plain on her face.

After a time, an old woman shows up. She is bent slightly, dressed in the same kind of simple garb, this one blue. She walks gracefully and has a bit of pale blue cloth tied around her head, from which escape strands of silvery hair. Her face is carved with years and years of living. She lifts her head for a moment, peers into the trees, and Frederick notices her eyes. So blue they are nearly one with the sky. He has seen those eyes somewhere.

And is he noticed? He does not know.

The woman drops her gaze and says, in a voice that

creaks rather than glides, "Little Miss Muffet, it is time for your shift in the streets."

"Oh, yes," Miss Muffet says. She wraps the bowl and spoon in the folds of a gray cloth and rises to her feet. "The sea is lovely today," she says, and with that, she leaves.

Frederick releases himself from the ball and follows her back along the line of trees. At one point, she looks up but does not seem to see him. She has the loveliest smile, precocious and challenging all at the same time. She does not seem to know that someone is watching her or following her, and she does not seem to even care.

Miss Muffet moves into the streets, takes a tin cup from one of the other beggars, and positions herself on a corner between two buildings, which Frederick can see clearly from where he is waiting.

He watches her for a long time.

And as he watches, it is with this knowing: he will return. She is much too fascinating a person not to observe. How can a child with seemingly nothing be so cheerful and full of joy and life? At least in Fairendale Frederick had a home and a mother and father and sister. A family. The woman who called this girl to the streets is much too old to be her mother. And it appears that she has no home. What does she have, then?

Frederick remains until Miss Muffet returns to the collection of people sitting or lying down on blankets of all shapes and sizes and colors. She lays her head on a pile of rags, curls herself into a ball, and closes her eyes.

Frederick's body aches again.

He returns to the spider den and is glad to know that the spiders are still sleeping.

Good. He will do it again tomorrow.

It is early morning, and King Willis is already awake. He has been ordered by Yasmin, who calls herself his advisor, to eat, sleep, and carry out his entire existence in the throne room (though King Willis, early on, convinced her to amend the eating portion of her command; no one is comfortable eating on a wooden platform or in a cold golden throne. A proper table with a comfortably padded chair makes for a much more enjoyable meal.).

But King Willis, after what he saw in the mirror last evening, has slept not a wink.

This morning, he has been unable to take his eyes off the mirror. His gaze is intent, as though he expects to see whatever it was he saw yesterday—a man flying into the invisible barrier of glass, sliding to the floor, disappearing.

Did he see it, or was it a trick of the imagination, a trick of the mirror, a trick of whoever controls this mirror?

King Willis glances back at the throne. It glows a soft violet color. He shivers. He is waiting for its curse to take effect, to steal back the pieces of himself he has regained, but he is still in control of his mind. His true self is not curled up in a corner, silenced by a force stronger than his own willpower, as it was for so many, many years.

Hc is glad. And frightened. And glad.

Perhaps he will be strong enough this time to resist the curse. Perhaps he will, at last, be able to do some good. Perhaps the world will be all the better for it.

But is he in control of his mind? He *did* see a strange man in the mirror. King Willis's eyes slide back to the mirror. What does he see now?

Himself.

He is a large man, but not as large as he used to be. He looks impressive, imperial even. King Willis straightens his back, presses a hand to the bronze bear that holds his royal robe together at the neck. He lifts his chin.

He looks like a king.

A king without his people.

King Willis's shoulders slump. He must find a way to

release the imprisoned children, to smooth over relations with their parents, to apologize for all the ways he has wronged so many of those he pledged to serve.

It is good for a king to apologize. He knows this. But still the thought of it dries out his throat.

He coughs. He squints. He understands.

Yes. The face he saw in the mirror yesterday felt familiar because he passed it every time he walked down the hallway with the paintings of past kings. The man in the mirror was a king—not his father, but someone else.

The man in the mirror was the king from whom King Sebastien stole the throne of Fairendale: The Good King Brendon.

But this is impossible. King Sebastien killed the Good King Brendon. It is why King Willis, today, sits on the throne instead of a descendant from King Brendon's family. It is why Fairendale has become what it is today. It is why…

His father, too, died, and yet he, too, is in a mirror.

King Willis swallows hard. The face of the former king looked familiar for another reason: it was the face of Cook, with a few slight adjustments—a stronger jaw, smaller eyes, a slightly larger nose.

He must find her, ask her what she knows.

But before he can move to do just that, the mirror

flashes and pops, and then there are sounds of struggle and sword fight. King Willis spins on his heel. Two men, facing one another, slashing at each other. Two men who drop their swords and wrestle instead. Two men who are kings.

King Willis rushes to the mirror.

"Father?" he says, but his father does not seem to hear him. He is shouting insults at the other man. King Willis watches, mesmerized.

Could this be a dream? It is possible. The nights King Willis sleeps and dreams, those dreams are filled with all sorts of impossibilities: his son, a blackbird; dragons, arranged in an army; his brother, returned.

And now this: King Sebastien and King Brendon, sparring again.

Two people, once dead, living again—in a mirror?

"Father!" King Willis says. He is afraid to touch the mirror, afraid the image will vanish. So he watches instead, helpless to do anything. They are locked together, as though they are embracing, but their faces are anything but kind.

King Willis spins on his heel. He must find Cook. He must bring her here, while the image is still visible—if it is, in fact, visible and is not simply the product of an overly exhausted mind.

What King Willis does not know about this throne room is that Yasmin has covered it in a spell—a spell to keep him in it. The spell, however, no longer works on him (it worked only once, in fact, when he first tried to escape); if it did, he would slam into an invisible wall any time he attempted escape. But because he does not meet the violence of an invisible wall, he suspects nothing of this Detainment spell beyond a small niggling question in his mind, a memory of his first attempt at escape.

Spells no longer apply to King Willis, thanks to Cook's enchantment on the pot in which his soup is cooked every night. Her spell negates any other spell. King Willis is well protected now.

He bursts out into the hallway to find that it is empty. He calls for Garth.

"Where is Cook?" he says as soon as the boy appears. His voice is high-pitched and agitated.

Garth shakes his head. "She is gone," he says.

"Gone?" King Willis says. "Gone where?"

Garth shrugs. "I do not think she said. But we can ask Calvin."

King Willis follows Garth to the kitchen. A small boy is stirring a pot of oatmeal that smells of cinnamon and apples. He turns when they enter. He bows. "Your Majesty," he says. He has such sorrowful eyes that King

Willis finds he must blink rapidly to clear the blur from his own.

"Where did Cook go?" King Willis wastes no time, and, in fact, there is no time to waste. Yasmin is, as they speak, heading toward the dining hall. She is unaware that King Willis is not deterred by her Detainment spell, and there is no telling what she will do once she finds out.

"She was Summoned," Calvin says. His voice cracks. He is so young—nearly as young as Prince Virgil. King Willis blinks his eyes again.

"Summoned?" King Willis feels like his old foolish self, repeating the words of people. He shakes his head to clear it. "By whom?"

"I do not know," Calvin says. "She said there is something she must do."

King Willis stares at him.

Calvin shrugs. "I do not know what it is."

King Willis feels the words piling up inside his throat, and when he opens his mouth, they shove out: "I have seen something in the mirror." His voice is low, measured, careful.

The boys stare at him, their mouths slightly agape. Their eyes are wide. They do not say a word.

King Willis is unsure whether he can say more. He looks from one of the boys to the other and back again.

No. He cannot let them know he has lost his mind.

So he says, "I will be awaiting my breakfast." Words that sound like a king. But not quite. Gentler, softer, kinder.

He turns and moves back toward the dining hall, where he enters in silence, sits at the head of the very long dark walnut table, and hardly notices Yasmin's entrance only seconds later, hardly feels her black eyes upon him, hardly hears the boy racing down the hall into the throne room and the other boy shoving through the dining hall doors to deliver a pot of cinnamon apple oatmeal.

The world has turned upside down, and King Willis does not know if he can stand.

Bryce, the queen of the dragon land of Daron Valley, which is slightly north of Lincastle all the way to the east, where the land meets the sea, is missing an egg.

Many months ago (a dragon egg takes a little more than a year to hatch) Bryce laid two eggs under some rotting plants, which was just as she had been directed by the elder black dragon of her land, the one practiced in dragon births and caring for young dragons. Ordinarily a black dragon lays her eggs and leaves them to hatch on their own and care for themselves, but Bryce is a queen. She is given leniency to tend her babies, though someone else will tend them once they hatch.

But she was sleeping one moment and woke the next to find that one egg was missing.

And now she is angry.

She is still a young dragon by dragon terms—one hundred fifty-three years old—so her anger is a pulsing, fiery, overwhelming one. (The emotions of dragons tend to even out as they grow older; anger is no longer such a danger. But Bryce has not yet lived long enough to tame hers.)

Her people have been looking for this egg. She has been guarding her remaining one, night and day, day and night. She is growing weary. She will have to enlist someone else to help while she sleeps.

But who else? Is there anyone she can trust? How does an egg disappear from its dragon mother, with no sign pointing to the thief, no sign to even prove that an egg existed at all?

She had a difficult time convincing her people that it did, in fact, exist. A dragon mother does not go around boasting about the eggs she has laid; she is modest and secretive. The fewer who know about such eggs, the less danger might befall those eggs. In the boasting, predators might overhear, humans might take notice and hunt them, and other dragons—particularly those who would like to see the throne of Daron Valley in hands other than hers or her heir's—might destroy them.

Bryce's mouth goes dry with this thought. Is this what happened to her egg? Did one of her dragons destroy it?

The lack of sleep is taking a toll on her mind. She wraps her body around the rotting plant that hides her remaining egg and closes her eyes. But sleep does not come.

She turns, curls, turns, curls, turns. At last, someone interrupts her from her futile attempt. Bryce raises her head, lumbers to her feet. Her second-in-command stands before her. "They have returned," Bryce says, and she hopes it is with good news this time.

The dragon dips his head, and she can tell—she can feel—that he comes bearing only bad news. She can already feel the fire gathering in her belly before he finishes his words. "We cannot find the egg, Your Highness," the dragon says in a sorrowful voice. Or is that fear twisting his tone? Does he fear what she will do? Does he fear what she has done the last several times he told her the egg cannot be found?

Black dragons only lay eggs every one hundred

twenty years. It is too long to wait for an heir, though black dragons also live the longest out of any of the other dragon tribes.

Bryce lifts her head, gazes into the too-blue sky, and roars long and loud. Her roaring sends a plume of fire, followed by gray smoke, into the air. She does not care that others—perhaps even people—will be able to locate them, does not care that she will be heard, does not care, does not care, does not care.

She must have her egg back.

And not simply because she is the young dragon's mother but because if the egg hatches, if the dragon growing within it lives, Bryce will be all the more weakened by her child's absence from her.

It is how the blood of royal dragons works.

Bryce returns her eyes to her second-in-command, who looks simultaneously angry, afraid, and apologetic. She says, "I will find my egg. And whoever has it will die without mercy."

And she means it.

The Huntsman—who is really Theo, the magical boy whom King Willis of Fairendale (under the curse of the throne—it is all very complicated) sent his men to capture by way of imprisoning all the children of Fairendale in hopes that he could find the magical one—places some sticks on a fire. He and the Enchantress have stopped for the night in a clearing of woods near Fairendale. Every time they pass his homeland, he aches to see what has become of it, what has become of its people and its children. Because of him.

But he is on a larger mission. He will save the children. He only hopes they will all forgive him for beginning this tragic circumstance in the first place.

Theo glances toward the cages of blackbirds in the cart. The missing one still bothers him immensely. How many children remain to be captured? Sixteen? And then the boy they found who disappeared again?

This quest is taking much longer than he and the Enchantress anticipated.

He is growing somewhat alarmed at the now-visible exhaustion of the Enchantress. She sleeps more and more of late. They have been leaving camp later and making camp earlier these last few days. In fact, the sun has not even gone down yet, and already they are stopping for the night.

Theo wonders why she does not let him lead their way. She did so once, when she was especially tired. But she seems unable to surrender control. He would do just as well. He knows where they are going. He has grown intimately familiar with these lands in their weeks—has it been months yet?—of travel.

There is also the problem of the looking ball. One child at a time. It is the most inefficient use of their time and energy. It is as though someone is trying to exhaust them.

For what? Is something happening about which they know nothing? Are there forces gathering that might need him and the Enchantress to be weak and weary?

The thought makes him shudder. He glances toward the Enchantress's tent. He knows where she keeps her looking ball. If she sleeps, he might be able to steal it.

Theo creeps toward the tent. He moves the flap in barely discernible stages. At last, it is open enough for one eye to peer inside. He sees the Enchantress, her face relaxed and lovely in sleep. Her breath is heavy and even. He sees her shiny golden shoes, just beside the bed.

He will have to be completely silent. He will have to hold his breath, even.

He crawls on his knees, into the tent, careful not to let the flap rustle. He does not even know if the looking ball will show him anything, but he must, at least, try.

The Enchantress does not stir as he takes her left

shoe, locates the miniature looking ball, which resembles a speck of dust—is it dust? No, this is a looking ball—and crawls back out of the tent. When he reaches the fire, he uses his staff—which is a pencil he keeps tied to his belt, along with a notebook in which he writes every night to record their progress, his concerns, and, more frequently of late, his feelings—to enlarge it. He places it on the ground in front of him and touches the tip of his staff to the glass.

Nothing happens.

He tries again. Still nothing.

Again he touches his staff to the glass. Nothing.

Theo feels like roaring his frustration, but he stops himself in time. The Enchantress would surely wake, and he cannot have her find him like his. With her looking ball in his hands. It would be the end of everything.

Rather than give up, however, Theo sorts through all the information stored in his mind. He used to sit in the back of his family's kitchen while Arthur taught the magical girls of Fairendale. Boys are not taught magic; it is dangerous in the land for a boy to have magic, since magic is the one requirement for ruling the throne of Fairendale. Arthur and Maude had urged Theo to keep his magic a secret.

Which Theo had done. Until one day he did

something foolish: accidentally used his magic to paint a face on a wooden puppet. Well, specifically, he used his magic to pluck a flying puppet (sent flying by his sister and her best friend, Mercy) from the air in order to give it a proper face. Prince Virgil saw and told his father about the magical boy. And so began this tragic tale.

Theo rubs his chest. Prince Virgil had been his best friend. But he had betrayed Theo. And the knowledge pressed into a tight, black ball in the pit of Theo's stomach.

He turns back to the looking ball. He knows a looking ball only works for its owner. But the Enchantress said that she did not own this looking ball; it simply appeared in her home one day.

What does that mean? Is she the first to use it, or does it belong to someone else entirely?

And if the latter is the case, why does it not work for him? If the looking ball is not faithful to its original owner, why would it deny him a look?

Theo swallows another frustrated growl. He touches his staff to the ball, but, of course, nothing happens. It remains a glass ball.

"Why are you taking us on such a circular route?" He hisses the words. He cannot help it. His frustration is too large and consuming.

The ball does not answer.

"You show us spiders and eggs and all manner of mysterious things." Now he is talking simply because he is lonely. "How do we know you do not lead us astray?"

Theo could very well record all of this in his journal, but for some reason, he feels better saying the words aloud, to the ball. He can almost imagine a person on the other side of it, listening. Theo has a twin, born the same day he was. He has not seen her in at least a moon; he does not even know if she is alive, though he still retains his magic, which is a good sign. In the land of Fairendale, if one magical twin dies (and most twins are born with the gift of magic, though not all), the other loses his or her magical abilities. It is a mysterious thing; they are two individuals, but their magic is linked. It is stronger than other magic. Some say that twins are the only sorcerers and sorceresses who can become Mages—the highest order of magical people, who are permitted the privilege of gifting others with magic.

Stories tell of Mages, but Theo has never met one. He does not know if they exist. Some stories are just stories.

"Why?" Theo's attention turns back to the ball. "Why?" He is surprised to note that his vision is blurry. He blinks his eyes rapidly and glances toward the birds—

the children—in their cages. They sleep soundly. The egg is nestled between two of them. An egg. For what?

Theo glares at the looking ball. He would like to demand some answers, but he knows it is useless. Besides, he will have to return the looking ball before the Enchantress awakens.

When he takes the looking ball back in his hands, Theo's frustration is so great that he nearly heaves it into the trees. But he stills his hand and sneaks it silently back into the tent of the Enchantress.

For a moment, he stands in the doorway, looking at her. He watches her eyes flutter as though she is dreaming. He wonders what her dreams look like. Does she see the same things he sees? Does she see birds and chaos and fire?

He hopes not. He hopes she sleeps much better than he does.

Theo turns away and makes his bed among the sleeping blackbirds.

Perhaps someday the ball will show him his sister. It is his last thought before he falls into a restless sleep, haunted by dragons and kings and a crone with piercing blue eyes.

Goodbye

After ensuring that the final Grace was alive and well, Kadesh and Bregdon slipped away, deeper into the woods where they could talk candidly without fear of being overheard by, particularly, Good Cheer, who did not like the djinn at all. No matter how many times Bregdon had explained that she would not be a Grace without the help of the djinn, Good Cheer did not care to change her opinion. The djinn was not welcome in her cottage. Bregdon would have enjoyed a cup of tea after such an intense battle, but he did not even attempt to ask.

Good Cheer was obstinate, to say the least.

"Well," Bregdon said.

"It was a satisfying final act of magic," Kadesh said. His eyes were sad. Bregdon wondered if he would miss the magic. He thought it likely. When one has lived with the gift of magic all one's life, it is difficult to part with it. It was the struggle of every parent in the realm of Fairendale: They could give up their magic to bear a child or they could keep their magic and remain childless. (Though, of course, several break the rules; magic is highly unpredictable in certain cases.)

For djinn, it was different. They could either have freedom or they could have magic.

"You are sure you want to do this?" Bregdon said.

Kadesh tilted his head. "I would rather not remain a slave," he said, and Bregdon felt the words spear his chest. If he had not Summoned Kadesh, the djinn would not have to make this decision. But what if someone less kind, more inclined to power, discovered Kadesh's true name and stole his freedom again?

It was better this way.

"Well, I gave you my word," Bregdon said. "I do not intend to break it."

Kadesh nodded. "Will it hurt, do you suppose?"

Bregdon swallowed hard. "Magic is part of your essence. I imagine it will feel like a stripping apart."

Kadesh cast his eyes to the ground but said nothing.

"You will never be a slave again," Bregdon said. "Pain is worth the freedom, is it not?"

"Yes." Kadesh whispered the words. He cleared his

throat. "Though I did not ask to be a slave in the first place."

"Who made you one?" Bregdon said. It was a question that came chained to his thoughts of Kadesh, but he had been too afraid, until this moment, to ask.

Kadesh shook his head. "I do not even remember," he said. "It was a long time ago, back when this land did not have so many people."

Bregdon knew the djinn was very old; the history books did not record the plight of the djinns; it was not the way of the powerful. They did not give space to servants. But he would write the story. He would add it to the Book.

"How will you do it?" Kadesh said. "With your magic?"

Bregdon said, "With the Old Man's Great Book."

Bregdon felt the djinn's eyes on him, but he studied his hands. At last Kadesh said, "You do not have a copy of the Old Man's Great Book." His voice had risen slightly, and when Bregdon raised his eyes to the djinn's, he saw that they flashed once again.

The djinn did not believe him.

Bregdon said, "I do not need a copy. I wrote it."

Kadesh stared at him as though he had never seen Bregdon before. "You…" What words he might have said trailed off, an unfinished question.

Bregdon straightened. His voice lowered. "I am Bregdon Lael Amidaeus, prophet of White Wind, author of the Old Man's Great Book." His words shook. It was the least he could do for a djinn whose name he knew: give the djinn his own name. Now it, too, could be used for Summoning, for truth telling, for Visions. Kadesh and Bregdon were both bound one to another, though Bregdon was about to break Kadesh's binding. So it would only be Bregdon, bound to Kadesh. A one-sided stitch. The tables turned.

Kadesh stared at him. "Bregdon Lael Amidaeus," he said in a whisper, as though trying out the name.

Bregdon nodded. They spoke without speaking. Kadesh lifted his hand. Bregdon pressed his palm to the djinn's.

"All my life, I thought men were not to be trusted," Kadesh said. He shook his head. "And now here you are. Bregdon, prophet of White Wind, author of the Old Man's Great Book." The djinn knew not to use Bregdon's other two names; ears could overhear them, and then another would have absolute power over the prophet. The djinn laughed, and the sound danced between them.

"You will have a good life," Bregdon said. "I know it."

Kadesh nodded. "And you will live again?"

"It is unknown," Bregdon said. "But worth the risk."

Kadesh's eyes turned glassy. He said nothing else but straightened his shoulders. Bregdon straightened his as well.

"Ready for your transformation?" Bregdon said, and Kadesh grimaced but nodded.

"I am, Old Man," he said.

Bregdon smiled at the familiar term. He did not mind being called an old man; it was true. And perhaps he would live longer, too. Did he want to?

What he wanted did not matter. What mattered was what was needed from him to protect the realm, to ensure its restoration, to save the people.

It was what had always mattered.

Bregdon took a deep breath and said, "Well. This is goodbye, then."

Kadesh smiled. "Not goodbye, Old Man. Until next time."

Bregdon closed his eyes and said the words of the most powerful spell he knew, the one that would transform and unbind and strip away magic all at once. He felt his own magic burning his fingertips. He held his staff tighter. He would not let go. If he let go, the enchantment would fail.

He could not fail Kadesh. Not again.

The moment before he died, Bregdon opened his eyes. The djinn stood in front of him, bonds broken, skin a honey-brown color, eyes of the strangest gold.

He was no longer blue. The enchantment worked. Bregdon's breath whispered out of him.

"It is done," he said, and the blackness swallowed him whole.

Declaration

As soon as he is certain that all the spiders in his den are asleep (there is something about the way a spider pack breathes during sleep; he spent quite a long time listening to it yesterday, when he returned from his exploration. He knows it, now, for what it is.), Frederick steps out into the early morning sunshine. He is surprised that he is not more tired than he feels; after all, he has not slept, other than a short nap during the hunting last night, since he hatched.

His short nap disoriented him. He dreamt he was a boy again, and when he was startled awake by the winning capture—a hatchling caught what looked like a wild boar this time—he was disappointed beyond words.

There is nothing he can do about this skin he wears, and the despair is beginning to take its toll on him. He walks slower, he limps more, he stands out more.

He must find Miss Muffet. He must have some of her joy. He must blend back in with the others.

Miss Muffet is in the same place, sitting on her small stool, eating out of her bowl.

This time the old woman who called her yesterday is sitting with her. Frederick balls himself up, wraps the silk around most of his body (leaving his man-spider face), and hangs lower this time. He listens.

"Why do you always come here?" the woman says as she looks out on the shimmering sea. Frederick keeps his eyes focused on Miss Muffet's shining face.

The girl smiles. "I like the smell of the sea," she says. "It smells a bit like hope."

Frederick inhales. The sea smells salty, fishy, like dirt and water and sea creatures are all mixed up as one, which is precisely what the sea is.

The old woman looks at Miss Muffet. Her eyes are very wrinkled, and her hair, uncovered today, is stringy, framing the sides of her face. Her clothes hang off her body, like crumpled rags.

"We might have to leave this land," the old woman says.

"I know," Miss Muffet says. "I will miss it very much."

"It has not treated us kindly," the old woman says.

"And I would rather you have safety than this halfway living of our current existence."

"It is not halfway living." The girl looks up into the branches, her gray eyes searching for something. Frederick tries to make himself smaller. Has he grown in the two days since he hatched? It feels as though he has. He closes all but two of his eyes. The eyes that wear the human spectacles.

"Look at the sky," Miss Muffet says. "It is such a beautiful color." Frederick looks up. The sky is the same color as her eyes, so he supposes it can be called beautiful, though it is not the color of beautiful skies. The girl continues. "The ocean is sweet and breathtaking. My life here has been…magical."

The old woman looks at her with pain in her eyes. But she smiles anyway.

They are silent for a long time. And then the girl says, "They might not want a girl like me." It is the first time that Frederick has seen her look anything close to troubled.

He shifts, and a branch cracks. Both the woman and the girl look straight up, and he shrinks again, trying to make himself as small as possible—a monstrous spider hiding among pink-leafed trees.

"They want all the children," the woman says,

looking down at last. "You would clean up well. I do not think the girls of the village poor will be exempt from the king's command."

Frederick senses something amiss, something dark, something just off to the left. He looks there. He sees a man, watching Miss Muffet and the old woman. When he looks upon the man, he feels a strange vibrating alarm, one that says: Danger.

The man's green eyes study the girl with what Frederick can only describe as hunger.

Hunger for what?

Miss Muffet and the old woman continue to speak, and Frederick continues to watch the man watching them, until Miss Muffet mentions Fairendale, and he hears the fear ring out into the air. It trembles through the trees. It shakes his sac.

"The king of Fairendale is a terrible man," Miss Muffet says.

The old woman turns to the girl. "Have you learned so little in our time together?"

Miss Muffet casts her eyes to the ground. She says nothing.

"They say the king is a terrible man," the woman says. "But I do not think all is as it seems in that land. I met the king once. He was not his father."

"You met the king once?" Miss Muffet says. The lilt has returned to her voice. The fear is gone. Frederick glances toward the man, who has disappeared. He does not know if that is better or worse.

"On one of my travels," the old woman says. "I was looking for another land." She chuckles.

"Did you already have me then?" Miss Muffet says.

Frederick thinks that perhaps he was mistaken about the woman being too old to be Miss Muffet's mother, until the old woman says, "I had not yet found you. But I was missing something even then; I just did not know what."

Miss Muffet smiles again and turns her gaze upon the sea. "And the king was not so terrible when you met him?"

"He was not so terrible as his father," the old woman says. "Sometimes people are raised in circumstances that make it difficult for them to be good people. And when there is no escape…" She pauses. "Evil is not born, it is made."

Frederick feels the words crash through him. There is the voice of his mother. There is her face. There is the ache.

He swallows all his pain so he will not give himself away.

The old woman's next words are soft, whispery. "Sometimes it is better to have love than wealth."

"All the time," Miss Muffet says, and she wraps her hand around the old woman's. Frederick's pain deepens.

After some time, Miss Muffet says, "I hope that I will come back to this land someday." Her face clouds, and then she lifts her chin and squares her shoulders and adds, "No. I will never leave this land in the first place."

The old woman looks surprised. "But there is a reward," she says.

Miss Muffet looks at the woman. "You said yourself that love is greater than wealth. Why would I give myself up for wealth? So that you could have a home that does not have me?"

The old woman smiles, a large and luminous one. She pats the girl's leg. "I thought you would say that all along, my dear." Her smile broadens, but this time it is for the sea. "I had to leave it up to you. But I hoped."

"I will not leave you," Miss Muffet says.

"And I will not leave you," the old woman says. They fall into one another's arms.

The man Frederick saw peering out from the trees is closer now, leaning in as though he is trying to hear. He is dressed in fine clothes—a clean white shirt that puffs at the collar; black breeches that billow out, catching on the breeze; and shining boots of the same color. He strokes a mass of black stubble on his chin. His green eyes sparkle. He turns and walks toward the village.

Frederick thinks about following him, but it is growing late. He must return to the den before he is discovered missing.

Once again, the spiders are still sleeping when Frederick slips inside the cave. No one even noticed he left.

So he will do it again tomorrow. And this time he will make his presence known to Miss Muffet.

Frederick falls into a deep and dreamless sleep so immediately that he does not see the eyes of Sparso snap open, fix on him, and close again.

The air inside the den, the air coming from one spider, shifts almost imperceptibly.

The Huntsman is gone when the Enchantress awakens. She has been sleeping more and more of late, and she knows he grows frustrated with their slowing pace. But what can she do? Magic demands much, and she expends most of hers day by day, hour by hour, minute by agonizing minute.

They traveled a bit farther last eve than they have been doing each day, but even with her spell to quicken them along, they have lost considerable time. She is not hurrying them enough for the Huntsman's satisfaction.

It is an impossible circle: the travel requires magic to hasten them, but the magic weakens her, which slows them down. Would it be better to travel with no Hasten spell? She would still grow weary; she protects them, too, from the beasts of the forests. She makes them invisible.

What is there to do?

The Huntsman has offered to take the lead while she sleeps in the cart along the way. But what of their protection? Would danger find them if she closed her eyes?

She did it once, and nothing happened. Perhaps it would be a good idea and would enable them to travel a bit faster.

The Enchantress folds her hands together and sits by the remains of the fire. What is wrong with her? Why has her exhaustion grown so ridiculously intense?

She does not know the answer to this question, but she suspects. Her magic is of a different kind now, ever since an old sorceress gifted her with something greater inside the Weeping Woods of Fairendale. She does not know how to control this magic; she does not even know if it is safe to use. The woman could have cursed her as easily as she could have gifted her. The lines between curse and gift grow blurry in magic.

This morning, the Enchantress's mind is fuzzy. She tries to remember where they are going. She cannot. So her mind is leaving her, too. What will happen next?

She pulls the looking ball out of her left shoe. It is slightly larger—barely; an untrained eye could not see it —than it was when she put it in her shoe. This trails a cold breath down her back.

Has someone tinkered with her looking ball?

She squints at it in the palm of her hand, trying to decide whether or not she should enlarge it. If someone cursed the looking ball, she will be vulnerable to that curse.

The Enchantress looks around, her eyes snagging on the Huntsman's pack. He left it on the ground, beside the fire, close enough for her to reach out and touch. Has the Huntsman been sneaking into her tent?

Where is he, anyway?

She shifts closer to his pack but eyes the speck of a looking ball in her hand. She is just about to enlarge it when she remembers: Lincastle. That is where she is going. And she has already been to Lincastle. Once? Twice? This she cannot remember, and it maddens her.

Much has maddened her in recent days. The exhaustion has begun to affect her mood. She snaps at the Huntsman, she chastises herself, she feels much more emotional.

Emotional enough to wonder what the Huntsman really thinks of all this. Emotional enough to wonder if he is who he seems to be. Emotional enough to wonder what it would be like to know more about him.

Emotional enough to worry that something is amiss.

Is she growing paranoid in her exhaustion? Why is it so difficult to trust someone like the Huntsman? He has only ever been kind to her.

The Enchantress glares at the pack. She knows he keeps a notebook in it. It would only take a moment. She could scan it, stuff it back, pretend that nothing was out of the ordinary.

No. She must not. The voice of reason is loud this morning.

But another voice joins it. *But what if he is leaving?*

Well, she must be prepared for that, must she not?

No. She cannot.

One of the birds is missing. What if he is responsible?

No. He could not be.

What if he controls the looking ball? What if he is playing a game?

The Enchantress picks up the pack. And then she drops it. And then she picks it up again, hoping that he will not return before she manages to see what is in it.

Just when she sticks a hand into the pack, a noise behind her startles her. She twists around, and there is the Huntsman. Of course. Her eyes widen, and her mouth opens.

He looks from her to the pack and back again. Her hand is still inside the pack, and she yanks it out as though whatever is inside burned her flesh. She *is* burning, but it is not from the pack. It is from the shame of being caught doing something that would anger her considerably, if she caught the Huntsman doing the same thing.

"You have my pack," he says. It is not a question. His eyes are unreadable. He has always been a mystery to her. But his breath hitches.

"I was moving it," the Enchantress says, but her voice shakes. She knows he will be able to perceive she is not telling the truth, even if he, by some miracle, did not see her hand inside it. "I did not want the fire to get it. It was careless to leave it so close." She will turn this around, pin it on him.

"That is why your hand was inside it," the Huntsman says. Still his eyes are unreadable, closed to her. He does not look angry, but she knows him well enough to see the tight clench of his jaw. He is trying not to let her see just how angry he is.

They had come so far, and she has ruined it all now.

Well, the damage is done. She may as well add to it.

She lifts her chin. "What do you keep in here?" she says. The pack is light, as though there is nothing but air. But she has watched him take things from it—notebooks, cloth pieces, a large ball of twine, even goblets and plates.

And when she stuck her hand in it, she felt something hard and jagged, like a weapon of some kind or another. But the pack does not reflect the weight of a weapon.

The Enchantress shakes the pack in the air, and the Huntsman bounds toward her. She tosses it on the ground so that he will not meet her, will not touch her, but he does not move toward the bag, he moves toward her, and, in a flash, she has her staff ready and waiting. The Huntsman takes one step back, and now she can read his eyes.

Hurt.

"You think I would harm you," he says. "You think…" He does not say more, but there is more in his voice, a sorrow like none she has ever heard before.

She turns away from him. It is the only thing left to do. "No," she says. Her shoulders drop for a moment, and then she squares them, turns back to the Huntsman, and says, "I only wondered what is in your pack."

"You only have to ask," says the Huntsman. He turns over the pack and shakes it.

There is a journal and a charcoal pencil and the beautiful crystal goblets they used during their supper in the woods not so long ago. There are the plates, a couple of tin cups, a fur. It is a large fur.

"What is that?" she says.

"The fur I made you," he says.

"You already gave me a fur cape."

The Huntsman stares at his feet. "I saw you shiver in the land of White Wind. I thought the first one I made was not warm enough. So I made another."

There is no weapon.

They do not say anything for quite some time, and then the Enchantress says, "How does it all fit in your pack?"

The Huntsman shrugs his shoulders. "It is a magical pack," he says.

She has never heard of such a thing, but it is fascinating. She wants to know how it is made. She comes closer to him and peers at the pack in his hands. She looks at him before touching it.

"All you have to do is ask," he says, again. He holds

the pack toward her.

She hesitates before taking it, and when it is in her hands, she says, "How do I know you do not have the missing bird in here?"

The Huntsman stares at her, as though trying to discern whether she is jesting or not. She wishes she were.

He shakes his head and rubs his hand over his chin. "You do not," he says. "But you can see for yourself."

The Enchantress feels around in the pack. There is nothing else inside it. She nods once and hands it back to the Huntsman. His eyes are so sorrowful that she cannot keep looking at them. She knows what they say.

After all this time, you still do not trust me.

She would like to tell him that she trusts no one, that she has always been this way. People have always failed her, since she was very young. Her mother most of all.

The Enchantress turns away.

As she has always done.

Something is wrong with the king. Garth can see it, but more than that, he can feel it. The king has, since yesterday, been staring at the magic mirror inside the throne room. What did he see? He told Calvin and Garth he had seen something, but he has not yet said what.

Garth tried to see it. After the king told him last eve, he slipped into the throne room while King Willis and Yasmin dined. He saw nothing in the mirror, only his own reflection.

Still the king stares, turning his head this way and that, contorting himself upside down, peering down his nose at it. King Willis sees nothing but the mirror.

There is nothing in it.

Garth has decided it is time to take the king's mind off the mirror and turn it elsewhere. He can be of help in other places, and Garth has seen the change that has taken place in the king. He knows the throne was cursed. He knows, too, that Cook's pot keeps the curse from working this time.

This will be to his advantage when Garth approaches the king and petitions him to free all the children in the dungeons beneath the dungeons. Garth has a looking glass inside his room in the castle—not a magical one, only an ordinary one—and last night he stood before this looking glass and practiced his speech.

He practiced it quietly, though Calvin is the only castle staff member who remains to overhear it. The other hundred or so servants fled the castle when the village people stormed it and stole the prince.

The hallways are so empty and dark. Garth has not been able to manage lighting all the torches. It is a job for two people, one to light and one to extinguish—and he has other, more important things to do.

Such as petition the king.

He practices again, now, in front of his looking glass. His eyes are bright and shining. His face is open and earnest. His voice has dropped, and he likes the way it sounds, the authority it carries.

He has never done something like this before, and his hands shake merely thinking about it. But King Willis is different now. He will listen. He will let them go. Garth is sure of it.

Garth has not been to the dungeons beneath the dungeons. Calvin is the only one permitted, by way of a magical door that only appears for the one who is chosen. Or so the three blind mice say. But who are they? Garth still is not entirely sure he can trust them. But no one else has offered an explanation for the way Garth cannot see a door where Calvin can.

Calvin needs a key to unlock the prison doors where the children and countless prophets are kept. He has not located this key, despite multiple searches throughout the castle.

No one has asked the king.

That is what Garth will do. He will tell the king why he believes the children must be released and then he will ask the king for the key.

The prophet in the dungeons—Garth thinks his name is Yerin?—told Calvin that a book—the Old Man's Great Book—might help them locate the key. But Calvin has not located the book, either. The king is the most direct route to answers and solution, and Garth's hopes fly high.

Hope that the king will know where this key is. Hope that he will tell Garth. Hope that the children will be set free to return to their families and live their lives.

Hope that the sun will return to the sky.

Garth dresses in his best servant's attire, although it no longer fits all that well, since the tailor fled Fairendale castle with the first wave of the castle staff, back when King Willis, then under the curse of the golden throne, invaded the village in hopes of capturing all the children (Garth believes that the servants who left in this first wave, as he calls it, likely returned to their families in the village and helped them escape from whatever might come next; he remained at the castle, for reasons still unknown to him). The rest of the castle staff fled when the village people invaded the castle and stole food, supplies, and the prince.

His pants are too short. The arms of his jacket show too much of his wrists. A button has popped off the part that pulls across his chest. Garth is broadening as well as lengthening.

Well, it will have to do. His mother taught him how to be a king's page, how to fetch things when she needed them, not how to sew on buttons.

He misses his mother. He wonders, not for the first time, why he has not returned for her, why he remains here in this castle, with no reason or purpose. It would be easy to flee and go home. His mother remains in the village. He knows this because he hears from her every week. They have their very own pigeon that carts letters back and forth. This pigeon knows his mother's house and knows which window is his. His mail is delivered right to his windowsill. He leaves the window open every night, though the land of Fairendale has grown chilly in the days since the children vanished.

He reads every letter that comes.

It has been some time since he has sent a return letter; she is always asking about his eleven brothers and sisters. They are all missing—all but him. And Garth does not know if they are in the dungeons beneath the dungeons or if they are out in the world, hiding from the king.

If they are hiding, they could come back. If he could find them, he would tell them they have no reason to fear the king anymore.

If they are in the dungeons, they could be released.

He hopes they are not dead.

Garth looks at the letters piled on his bedside table. He swallows the guilt. He knows he should answer, but he cannot. He knows so little. He has been stalling—wait until he knows more.

Will he ever know more?

He must.

He must help set the children free, and then his mother will be comforted. Perhaps they can all live here, at the castle, and serve in various positions, now that the staff has fled. What would his mother think of that?

Garth straightens his back and lifts his chin, and, one more time, rehearses his speech while watching himself in the looking glass. He has a bit of a stutter, but he manages. Well, even.

He cannot say for sure what will happen when he is standing before the king, but here, in his own room, he feels confident. The king will listen. The king will let the children go.

Garth smooths his hair away from his eyes. It has grown longer, somewhat unruly, in the last few weeks. His mother used to cut his hair when he returned for a visit, but it has been so long since he has visited. He tried to cut it himself a few weeks back, but that only ended in disaster. He has not tried again.

It is time. He must move.

Garth spins on his heel, yanks open his door with a confident pull, and heads toward the king's throne room.

He only hopes the monster-woman isn't there.

The lost boys, a collection of six—three ten-year-olds and three eleven-year-olds—have been hiding out, unsure what to do about the one of them who went missing. One week and one day ago they were surrounded by a throng of fairies. These fairies came to take them to Never Land. The Lost Boys, as they have taken to calling themselves (once upon a time, they called themselves FLAT HEN, an anagram of the first letters of their names; this was much more entertaining, but they have lost two of their group and would now only be LA HEN, which, in their opinion, is not as funny. Besides, changing the name in that way would seem disrespectful to the ones who have gone missing, as though they were forgotten. We have been calling them lost boys for a while now, but they have only just discovered how perfect the description.), refused to accompany the fairies to Never Land. And the next thing they knew, the fairies encircled them, glowing bright and beautiful colors. It was mesmerizing, until the circle shifted and became nearly suffocating, to say nothing of the intensity of that fairy light. When the fairies finished their spectacle, the boys remained in the Wishing Woods of Lincastle, minus one.

Fineas.

The boys are despondent. First it was Theo, now it is Fineas. They do not know what to do. So they have been hiding away in this old, leaning shelter, where Theo first brought them after saving them from the king of Fairendale, who pursued a magical boy and, in his pursuit, decided to round up all the children of Fairendale, nonmagical included.

None of the Lost Boys has a bit of magic in him. Theo did.

For the eighth day since the disappearance of Fineas, Norman, who is ten, asks the group, "What are we going to do?"

"I do not know that we can do anything," Ernest says. "Everywhere is dangerous."

It is not that Ernest is a coward; he is simply stating the facts: everywhere *is* dangerous for these Lost Boys.

When you cross a fairy, it is the reality of your life ever after.

"We must find Fineas," says Henry, who is ten.

"Perhaps he left on his own," says Leo, who is eleven.

"He would have come back," August says.

"We must do something," Norman says again.

"What?" Leo says. "What is there to do?"

"We could venture into Lincastle," Henry says. "Search for him there."

"You think he went into Lincastle?" Ernest says.

"We saw the circle," August says glumly. "We saw the fairies, and we saw him disappear with them." He recalls the terror on Fineas's face; he had been standing right beside August. August does not want to ever see such a look of terror again, though he sees it all the time in his sleep. It is the thing that haunts his dreams.

"We have to do *something*," Norman says.

"Enlighten us then, Norman," Leo says.

They are all grumpy and tired and out of ideas. They have had this conversation—nearly exactly—for eight days. August is growing weary of it.

August was put in charge of the Lost Boys after Theo left them. They look to him for guidance, for what to do, and August hardly ever has an answer.

He is worried that the fairies will take them one by

one.

He is worried that he will be the last remaining. He has never done well on his own.

And perhaps this worry has plagued him so much and so often of late that he says something completely different in the course of this familiar conversation. He says, "They took him to Never Land."

The boys stare at him, but not one of them disagrees.

"If we want to find him, we will have to travel there," August continues. The possibility has been building in his mind for the last day.

"But how?" Leo says.

August shakes his head. This is the part he cannot seem to work out. "I do not know."

They sit in silence for a time.

Henry is the first to speak into their silent thinking. "Perhaps someone else would know how to get there," he says.

The boys look at each other.

Leo says, "What creatures are enemies of the fairies?"

The boys look at the ground. They all know which creatures are the enemies of fairies. They do not want to consider an interaction with these creatures.

Trolls.

In the realm of Fairendale, trolls can be troublesome

creatures, though not as troublesome as goblins; they do not take humans as slaves. They look similar in their repulsiveness, but that is where the similarities end. Where goblins are massive and green with a hooked nose, bulbous heads, and small, beady eyes that do not line up, trolls are marginally nicer to look upon. Most of them are large beings the color of stone—gray, usually—with squat, round noses, eyes that line up for the most part, and a shock of white or silver hair sticking up from the top of their head, generally tied with a bit of twine. They hunch when they walk, their arms nearly dragging the ground. They are slow and considered of inferior intelligence, though there are many who are intelligent indeed; they simply do not wish to be seen or acknowledged, having no interest whatsoever in the human world other than, occasionally, as a delicacy at their table.

Because of this, they are dangerous to engage.

But legend says that trolls have a particular dislike for fairies.

Lincastle legend also says that unicorns are enemies of fairies, but these boys are from Fairendale, and they have never heard the stories. Trolls are their only option, they believe.

The boys shiver.

August says, "We will have to be careful."

Leo says, "Fineas's life is worth it.

Henry says, "We must, at least, try."

Norman and Ernest nod.

They all look to August.

"We will have to do it just before daylight," August says. "So we can be sure of our escape."

He does not say that they can never be sure of their escape with trolls. Will the light streaming through the spaces between trees be enough to stop a troll? Trolls turn to stone if they are caught in the daylight. It will be risky. But they have survived risky before, have they not?

August is quiet for too long. Henry says, in a voice small and tight, "Do you think we can do this without Fineas?" Fineas, who was the rebel. Fineas, who had enough courage for all of them. Fineas, who dared and dreamed.

"And what about what we planned to do before Fineas…" Leo lets his voice trail off.

Before the fairies stole Fineas, the Lost Boys made a collective decision to return to the land of Fairendale, save Theo, and see that the rightful king—Theo, of course—was set upon the throne. They have reason to believe that Theo is the rightful ruler; he was born with magic, and Fairendale needs a new king. A king who is merciful and kind and justice-minded. A king who is for the people. A king who loves.

August's mind sorts through the two options. Theo has magic; perhaps he would be just fine.

But what of Fineas? They know only two things about Never Land: the first that when you live there, you never grow up; and the second: You can never leave.

Is their decision made for them, then? Will they all be captives of Never Land, instead of only Fineas?

"If it were one of us, Fineas would travel to Never Land," Henry says.

August nods. Yes. He would.

"He does not want to be there," Leo says, as though thinking out loud.

"We must save him, then," Norman says.

"So trolls," Ernest says, and everyone grows quiet, their courage faltering once more.

August knows it is his turn now. "We are the Lost Boys," he says. "We have survived these woods for more than a moon. On our own. Without parents or guardians or protectors. We can do anything." His voice grows larger and stronger as he speaks. He says it again: "We can do anything."

And he is shocked to find that he believes it.

They can do anything.

The boys nod and look at each other.

"We can do anything," they say.

They plan long into the night.

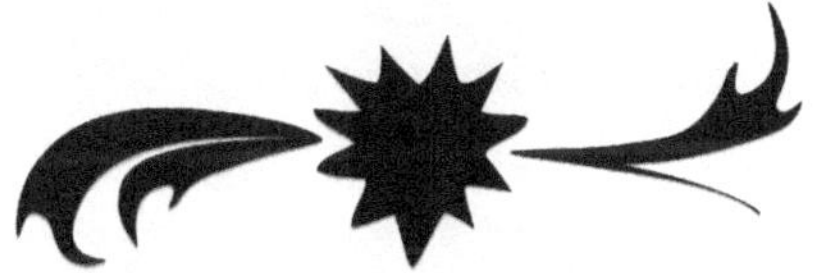

Haunting

Bregdon was, of course, given another chance at life. Who knows how many he would have; he made it his goal to live each one to its fullest. He checked in on the Graces, though they did not know it; he looked in on all the lands, though no one paid him much mind; he located the djinn, living with a rust-haired wife in the land of Eastermoor, two black-haired children sitting on his knee.

He lingered on Marion. She was an enigma. It was impossible, still, to tell whether he had done the right thing, bringing her back to life. He thought a visit might do her some good. But he never got the chance.

It did not take Bregdon long, in his observations, to see that the Grim Reaper was abnormally interested in Marion. Bregdon knew the rules of the Grim Reaper: the wraithlike horror could not enter homes without being invited, unless someone within it was dying. Bregdon knew Marion was safe, then. But still, the Grim Reaper trailed her, as though he knew something no one else did.

And this made Bregdon shiver.

What if?

Sometimes, rather than opening wondrous worlds, the words "What if" can be terrifying ones. Bregdon watched Marion, watched the Grim Reaper, watched the Black Eyed Beings and their odd interest in Marion. He saw Marion turn into a toad the Black Eyed Being she met on the streets of Lincastle. And he noticed the notch.

Ah. Her staff counted how many Black Eyed Beings were destroyed. That was something. A staff can be more than a medium for magic; sometimes it can communicate one's destiny.

Bregdon knew the woman suffered for not knowing why she had been brought back to life. Well, this would be a noble cause, would it not? Destroying the Grim Reaper's army?

Or would it? Bregdon did not know enough about the Grim Reaper. Would it be people she was destroying or simply undead spirits? How was a Black Eyed Being made?

Bregdon needed to learn more.

And he tried. But it seemed that the mysteries of the underworld were closed to him. So Bregdon decided, rather impulsively, to approach the Grim Reaper himself. He had nothing to fear; Bregdon had already died many deaths. The Grim Reaper had not taken him.

During one such vigil outside the cottage of Marion, when Bregdon watched the Grim Reaper watch the Evil Queen, Bregdon found his voice. "Why do you watch her?" he said.

The Grim Reaper whirled around, a whisper of cloak and bone. His skeletal cheeks lifted into a lipless smile. "Bregdon Lael Amidaeus, prophet of White Wind."

His name, spoken by the king of Death, sent a shiver through Bregdon. How did the Grim Reaper know it?

"I know every name," the Grim Reaper said.

Bregdon felt his shoulders relax, if only a little. So he could not do anything with the name; it would not be permitted.

"Soon I will be able to Summon anyone I like," the Grim Reaper said, as though he could hear every thought Bregdon had.

"No," Bregdon said. "It is not permitted."

If possible, the Grim Reaper's smile grew even more horrifying. "There is always a way," he said. The Grim Reaper's black eyes, bottomless, it seemed, fastened on

Bregdon. The air around them turned cold and icy.

The Grim Reaper said, "You see how my army grows?" and gestured to the space around him, which, before, had been empty, wide open, and now was filled with Black Eyed Beings. As far as Bregdon could see, there were souls, people, the living dead—whatever they were. Bregdon tried to breathe.

"It will not be long," the Grim Reaper said. "And then I will have all of the people." He tilted his head in a grotesque way. "But first I will take you."

He moved faster than was possible, and his people closed in around Bregdon. Bregdon knew it was risky, but he channeled all of his magic into the circle and released a blast of blinding light.

When he woke again, it was to life, but changed life. He could feel the fear, which would never truly leave him. He learned later that it had not been solely his One Last Great Act that had saved him from the Grim Reaper and the army of undead; it had been dragon fire in the lands of Morad, and the falling of the king's men of Fairendale castle. The Grim Reaper had taken his opportunity to add numbers to his army, rather than power.

But Bregdon knew he would be back, as he had promised. He would be back for all of them.

And when he came, what then?

Mysteries

Miss Muffet has returned to what Frederick has come to think of as her regular spot, if it can, in fact, be called that in the span of the two days he has been observing her. It seems as though she has spent more than two mornings here, he reasons, and so it could be called a regular spot. He hears his sister arguing in his head. *Two days of the same thing is nothing.* It almost makes him smile.

He left the spiders sleeping once more, after a fruitful hunt last night. He did not catch anything, but his brothers and sisters—brothers and sisters? Never!—did. He pretended to eat, and chewed on some leaves this morning. It all tastes the same to him. He is tired of being a spider.

But what can he do?

For now, he can pretend. He can meet this girl. He

can absorb some of her joy, some of her strength, some of her courage.

But plans change so quickly, in the blink of an eye. That is exactly what happens to Frederick. One moment he hears the footsteps, the next moment he turns to look, the third moment he recognizes the man with hunger in his eyes. The man who whispers to his partner, "We will turn her over to the king, and she will fetch us a pretty prize." The man who heads toward Miss Muffet.

She does not seem to hear him. She eats her mush and gazes on the sea, a tranquil picture of beauty and contentment.

The man will not have her. The king will not have her.

Frederick acts on an impulse. He drops himself down to just above Miss Muffet and says, "You must go. Run. Do not look back."

Miss Muffet nearly drops her bowl, but she has not yet looked up. And when she does, she screams. The bowl of mush spills on her lap, a gray stain on her faded red dress. Her eyes widen in horror.

In her haste to get away, escape from the monster, save herself from certain death by spider, Miss Muffet turns over the stool. And then she does as he commanded. She runs and does not look back.

In the place of Miss Muffet's footsteps, Frederick hears the feet of giants.

Giants? Is Lincastle home to giants?

He turns around and, with horror, witnesses a whole group of monstrous spiders, crawling on the ground, not even using the cover of the trees. People scream. Plates drop. Frederick's breath catches.

The army of spiders stops in front of him.

Demarek moves out from the rank. Her eyes are very sad, and Frederick feels a heaviness slide into his throat. "You must come with us, little one." Her voice is gentle, like his mother's turned when he was hurt.

Frederick fumbles for his courage. "My name is Frederick," he says. Demarek's eyes widen. She glances behind them at the mass of spiders and turns back to him, drawing nearer.

"Do not speak your name," she says. "You are a spider." Her eyes seems to say something more.

Do not tell them. Do not let them have a reason to kill you.

But do they not already have one? He has ventured out from the nest. The people have seen them.

Frederick eyes the spiders, trying to see if there is some break in their file where he might successfully slip through and escape. But there is nothing. He is surrounded. He is trapped.

The only place he could run is the Violet Sea, and he knows, on instinct, that he will drown in the waters. Spiders are not given the ability to swim—not even monstrous ones like him.

There is no way out. The truth nearly knocks all breath from his chest.

Mother. Father. Lilah.

He will never see them again.

"Please, Frederick," Demarek says, and the way his name rolls off her lips wraps around his throat and pinches. "Do not make this harder than it must be."

Frederick would like to revolt, would like to say what has been in his mind (these spiders are savages, they are monsters, that is all they have ever been and will ever be), but all the words get caught in his throat. Wisdom wins. He knows, from the look in Demarek's eyes, that these spiders are, without a doubt, cruel and sadistic.

Evil is not made, it is born.

His mother and father were wrong.

The old woman with Miss Muffet was wrong.

Frederick draws himself up to his full height, though he is nothing compared to the largest spider here. He says, "You are going to kill me, then?" He tries to speak the words bravely, but they shake out as though they have been gusted by the four winds at the same time.

He does not want to go with them only to die. He will die here, fighting them.

Demarek does not look at him when she says, "That is up to you. Sparso has ordered that you return." Her eyes are still pleading when she lifts them. They shift into their lovely blue. "Please."

Frederick wonders then how much she has done for him, how persistently she has pleaded for him, how greatly she has risked. She moves closer and lowers her voice. "They have been ordered to kill you if you do not come. And you are needed." These last words she whispers.

Needed?

Frederick is startled by her words. How does she know he is needed? The only thing for which he has ever been needed in his life of twelve years is cooking. He cannot cook as a spider. He cannot do anything much as a spider. Why would he be needed?

But Demarek is looking at him as though she knows what he is and who he is. And perhaps, just a little bit, he believes her. He *is* needed. If he is needed, he must live.

As he looks at Demarek, as he considers the possibilities—particularly this great possibility of being needed—her eyes turn to mirrors. He sees himself. And then her eyes become windows. He sees the lost children of Fairendale, some of whom he recognizes, some of whom are completely transformed. Some old crones, some recognizable boys, the tiny girl Lina, and even one who lives beneath the sea.

All his fellow friends and acquaintances. Needed.

Demarek's eyes return to their beady black. He knows he has not imagined it this time, and once the amazement has passed, he feels a wave of fear.

He takes a step back. "Who are you?" he says.

"I am a spider," she says. "Nothing more." But he can tell, by the way her words wrap around him, that she is more than a spider. Something much more.

"You must come with us," Demarek says.

Frederick looks back at the waiting spiders. Why have they been waiting for so long without moving? He blinks. Not one of them so much as shifts.

"What have you done to them?" Frederick says.

Demarek glances behind her again. "I believe we have stepped into a suspension of time. How fortunate."

Frederick shakes his head. He must be dreaming. It is too fantastical, even for this magical land. A spider who can do magic?

"You must come," Demarek says. Again.

"They will kill me anyway," Frederick says.

"Perhaps not," she says. "It is not yet decided."

"Then they will throw me in a cage, and I will never escape," Frederick says.

"One never knows the future, so why not at least try?" Demarek says.

So Frederick, after some minutes of thinking, says, "Very well," and a whoosh sounds around him. The spiders tremble with excitement. Time resumes.

"He will come peaceably," Demarek announces, and one of the spiders moves forward.

"Follow me," he says, in a low and menacing voice.

And Frederick does. He looks round once, to find Demarek, but she is no longer there, swallowed up by a wave of spiders. The streets of Lincastle are deserted, but Frederick sees the faces of the people, peering out their windows. They close their curtains when they notice the line of spiders moving.

Frederick cannot blame them; he would do the same.

And the pain of this truth nearly folds his legs.

But he limps on. He must endure. He must survive.

He is needed.

Yasmin stands in front of the magical mirror inside the Fairendale throne room, speaking to it. She has dismissed the king from the room (the first of his tests), allowed him a bit of freedom but with the stipulation that he will return here, in an hour's time.

She does not worry about what he might do in that time. He looked completely perplexed at the promise of freedom.

Yasmin narrows her eyes. "Come out, come out, wherever you are," she says. She circles the mirror, studying the back of it, peering into the glass, trailing her fingers over it.

She tries again. "I would like to see you. Please come out." She arranges her voice into the kindest, most curious, most accommodating one she can manage.

For several minutes this continues, her voice growing increasingly louder and more frustrated.

No one appears in the mirror.

Yasmin turns from the mirror and clenches her fists. What did she see in the mirror? Will she see it again? She has been over and over this, but she has found no answers.

Her frustration tastes bitter, like the food she tries every day, hoping that she will be able to taste it this time. Those who, like her, have been brought back to life not with magic but with science are not permitted the simple pleasures of life—such as tasting delectable food. This is speculation on her part, but it is a good theory.

Yasmin takes a breath and lets it out slowly. She must calm herself. She must convince whoever is in the mirror to show his face.

"I only want to see you," she says to the wall. Her back remains to the mirror, but a sound pulls her around.

The mirror flashes such a brilliant light that Yasmin must hold an arm across her eyes. When her vision recovers from the shock, she sees the man in the mirror.

A different man.

This one wears the robes of a prophet, in black. The hood is draped over his head, but Yasmin can see the white of his hair, which matches the white knots hanging from his chin and the patches on his cheeks. His eyes, peering out from beneath the hood, are a rich umber.

What is happening? First the golden-haired man, now this one. Where is Sebastien?

Yasmin takes one step toward the mirror. She says, "Who are you?"

"I am the man in the mirror," says the man. He folds his hands together and meets her eyes, only breaking her gaze once to look beside him, as though he is not alone. She looks, too, but she sees no one.

"You are not the man who used to look out from this mirror," Yasmin says.

"I have always been in this mirror, since the beginning."

Yasmin does not know what he means. The beginning of what? She says, "Where is the other man?"

"I am the man in the mirror," says the man, without answering her question. "I was the first man in the mirror." He is quiet for a moment, and Yasmin is about to say something when he says, "There are many here."

"Many?" Yasmin moves even closer to the mirror. She sees no one but this man, a prophet, apparently. "Where are they?"

"In this mirror," says the man.

"Why can I not see them?" Yasmin says.

"They are…" the man stares at the space beside him. "Indisposed."

A cold breath moves down Yasmin's back, but it is nothing compared to the wind that accompanies his next words.

"And I am coming for you."

She throws the red drape over the mirror and drops down to the steps of the platform.

What does it mean?

Many in the mirror. This man is the original. He is coming for her.

He is coming for her.

This last bit lingers in her mind. She stands to her feet, feeling more courageous now that the mirror has been concealed. She lifts a corner of the drape and peers at the glass underneath, waiting for the man to appear.

But instead, it is someone else.

Not King Sebastien. Not the one who says he has been in the mirror since the beginning. This is the golden-haired man. He looks like a king, too. One word escapes his mouth before some invisible force yanks him from view. "Help."

Yasmin lets the drape fall over the mirror again. She slams a hand against it. She roars—a decidedly feminine one. She takes a deep breath and releases it. She lifts the drape for the third time.

"Mirror, mirror," she says, and she has not even finished the second word before the man in black robes appears again, his eyes shining and hungry.

"You are frustrated," he says. "Understandably so."

"Where is King Sebastien?" Yasmin's voice is tight, pinched, angry. She is no longer fearful; this man cannot hurt her. He is trapped in a mirror. She would like to banish him.

"He is…sleeping." The same pause, the same satisfied look in his eyes. Yasmin very nearly hits the glass again, but she does not know if breaking the glass will release this man or not. She must not risk it. She keeps her hands pressed together, behind her back. She does not want him to see how he is affecting her.

Yasmin lifts her chin and says, "Tell me who you are."

"I already have. I am the man in the mirror."

"But you were not always a man in a mirror."

Something flickers in his eyes. It is the smallest, most inconspicuous flicker, but Yasmin sees it. Ah. There it is. His humanity.

He misses someone.

Yasmin waits.

The man says, "No, I was not always trapped in a mirror."

"Who are you?" Yasmin says again. Her voice is stronger now, resilient, authoritative.

The prophet stares at her for a moment, and then he says, "I am Folen, former prophet of Lincastle, father of Iddo."

The name jolts through Yasmin. Iddo, the man who created her.

The hatred is wildly fierce. She says, between clenched jaws, "I must speak to King Sebastien."

"You can speak to me," Folen says.

"No," Yasmin says. "King Sebastien and I are making a plan."

"King Sebastien has no business in this mirror," Folen says, and now his eyes flash, turning the shade of wet mud, like a storm is gathering. "This is my mirror."

"You want to be in the mirror?"

The words hang between Yasmin and Folen. The silence is thick and oppressive.

At last, Folen shakes his head. "No," he says. Something flickers in his eyes again, and Yasmin is sure she understands now. He misses his son. He misses her creator. He misses the man who could not let the dying die.

Yasmin tells him nothing of what his son has done. She would rather not talk about it at all. She says, "I would like to speak with King Sebastien." She adds, "Please," thinking that perhaps it might help.

Folen does not step aside, however. Instead, he says, "I can help you. I can even make you beautiful again. I know how."

The words wrap around her, alluring. She tries to ignore them, but there it is: beauty. What the world tells a woman she must be: beautiful. It is no different in any of the lands; a woman cannot be herself anywhere.

The words slide deeper, whispering, *What would King Sebastien think if he saw his mother standing before him, instead of this monster?*

The ache is nearly unbearable.

But Yasmin is strong. "I do not need beauty."

"Do you not?" Folen says, and his tone, his eyes, even, imply that he does not believe her.

"No. I do not."

Folen nods. "Very well, then. I suppose I cannot help you look living again."

He begins to turn away, and Yasmin would like to let him, but the words have lodged too deep. "Wait."

The prophet turns around, his lips curled into the tiniest of smiles. A satisfied smile. It almost makes Yasmin renew her determination to resist his wily ways. But her mouth has a mind of its own, and before she can stop it, the word is already out. "How?"

"All you need to do is find the Old Man's Great Book." Folen's eyes fasten on hers. "I know it is here. I can feel it."

"The Old Man's Great Book?" Yasmin says.

"It is the greatest book of enchantments the world has ever seen," Folen says. "A log of every spell in existence. The spells that will get you a kingdom, that will show you your missing pieces, that will reinvigorate your beauty."

"That will free you?"

The prophet only smiles.

"There must be a reason you are trapped in this mirror," Yasmin says.

"Perhaps." The prophet does not offer anything else.

Yasmin studies him, studies the eyes that resemble fresh mud, the hair like snow, the robes that cover him almost entirely. The robes of a prophet. Prophets can generally be trusted, but what about this one?

"Where would I find this book?" Yasmin says at last.

Folen shakes his head. "I only know that it is here. Perhaps you could start in the castle library." He pauses. "Or with the queen."

Yasmin stares at him for a moment and then looks down at her hands. They have a bluish hue. A black stitch, crooked and ugly, runs across the top of her right hand. Beauty and life. Is it worth it? How dangerous is this man, and will he be the only one free?

She will think of the questions later. For now…

"I will return with the book," she says. "And I will expect that King Sebastien is kept safe."

The prophet nods, his self-satisfaction clear in his eyes. Yasmin turns away before she can change her mind. She does not cover the mirror, does not glance back at the prophet, does not speak a word as she moves down the red carpet and out the throne room doors.

Had she looked back, she might have seen the dark

eyes of the prophet glowing violet.

A frightful, horrifying thing.

The dragons of Morad have called another council. The food shortage is getting dire. They do not know what they can do, besides taking their hunt into other lands and risking the wrath of the other dragon kings and queens, who are very territorial.

Dragons are mostly creatures who keep to themselves, but when someone invades their land—man or dragon, for good or ill—they get ferociously defensive. They will fight for their land until they have succeeded in keeping it untainted by outsiders.

The dragons of Morad know this. But the food in their lands—which includes not only Morad but a portion of all the forests that connect with Morad—has all but vanished.

They believe it is the work of dark magic. They would like to know if the situation is the same in other dragon kingdoms. They hope it is not—and yet, at the same time, they hope it is. If other kingdoms have lost their abundance as well, it means there is nothing wrong with their land, specifically, but something wrong with the entire realm.

There is strange comfort in suffering together.

"Only monsters remain in the woods now," says Larus, a blue-green dragon whose scales shift and shimmer according to his mood. Today they are more blue than green. Sad. "They are all I can find, for miles around."

"The woods would be better if we took all the monsters," says the red dragon with a cream-colored underside, Malera. "But…"

She does not have to finish her sentence; every dragon here knows that the dark creatures must be left alone. To eat them would be to risk picking up a curse that cannot be cured. Dark creatures contain dark magic, and dark magic is nearly always a curse.

It is unfortunate; the dragons of Morad would prefer to eat monsters instead of the lovely woodland creatures. But before, the woodland creatures had been abundant— much more abundant than monsters. Now it seems the monsters have multiplied.

"It is the monster at Fairendale castle," Blindell says, but they all ignore him. He knows they hear him; one of the dragons in their circle even glances at him before looking away.

For the last six days, Blindell has been imprisoned

inside a magic circle. Magic circles are helpful things when one wants to keep an enemy contained, but Blindell is no enemy. This is what he has been shouting periodically when dragons walk by his invisible cage. He is held by a curved wall, and there is hardly enough room to stand up or lie down. He certainly cannot spread his wings, which might give him some hope for escape.

He was placed here by a woman. A sorceress with golden hair and eyes the color of the sky at dusk. She called herself a protector.

He calls her an enemy now.

Blindell has never, at any other moment, wished more for his rider to show up. It is true that he resents her—perhaps even hates her—but he could use her powers now. If she has regained them. She had lost the use of her magic the last time she came to visit, when he injured her (no, he does not feel badly about it, though he sustained a gash in his leg as well; it is the law of a rider and the dragon linked to the rider. Whatever one does to the other, one does to oneself. It is supposed to keep them safe from one another, but what does he care?).

Perhaps she would not be able to help him, either.

Perhaps, instead, he should be on his best behavior, pretend the magic circle and his time imprisoned within it has changed him, prove that he is worthy, in his renewed state, of freedom. And once the dragons set him free, he can have his revenge.

Blindell glares at the circle of dragons, so close he can hear them, so close he can speak his mind and be heard as well, so close he could—

"Clearing the Weeping Woods of the monsters would surely bring the curse of dark magic upon us," Larus says.

"It could very well also bring the ruler of all the monsters," says the old dragon Oned. Blindell squints his eyes, trying to see, not for the first time, what color Oned used to be. He is so old he is gray now. Were his scales once yellow? Orange? A pale blue?

Blindell tries again: "The ruler of the monsters is a creature living in Fairendale castle." He knows it is futile; the dragons do not believe him. They do not know what he has seen.

Since the red-haired woman became his rider—a happenstance about which he is still quite angry—Blindell has had a strange ability to see things. When his mind wonders something—such as *Why are the woods so dark?*—the answer plays in a picture across his mind. He has seen the monster with her black hair and black eyes and blue-hued skin. She is not living, but she is not dead, either. She hovers between the two.

She is dangerous.

Larus is the only one who looks at Blindell again. He asks no questions, and though Blindell is frustrated by this complete lack of interest, he is also, to tell the truth, somewhat relieved. What would he tell the dragons if they were to ask him how he knows what he knows? He cannot admit that he has a rider; he cannot admit that he is tied so absolutely to another—a human. He has only ever wanted to destroy humans, after they killed his father and mother in the Great Battle and left him to be raised by his cousin, the king of Morad.

"Is there anything else that can be done?" says the old female dragon, Alvah, who once wore shiny red scales—Blindell remembers when she did; she was often kind to him and his father, who was a foreigner to the land of Morad—but now wears faded orange scales.

The dragons are quiet for some minutes. Blindell does not even try to insert his opinion. He knows they would not listen anyway.

"Hunt in other lands," Larus says. "But that would violate the dragon rules." One understood dragon rule among all the dragons in the realm is this one: No one takes food from another. They have their territories, their hunting grounds, and that is their allotment. It was done at the beginning of time.

Blindell nearly rolls his eyes at the old ways. Perhaps it is time to change some of them. Desperate times demand creativity and innovation. But he remains silent; he will let the dragons make their own decisions and live with the consequences.

Malera says, "It is hunt the evil creatures or die."

A heavy silence falls over the dragons again. This time Blindell cannot keep quiet.

"Or the people," he says. That would solve all their problems—at least the hunger kind.

They ignore him, as he expected. Blindell has been urging the dragons of Morad to eat the Fairendale people—for whom he has a particularly strong hate reserved in his heart—since the first desperate signs of famine began to show themselves in the lands of Morad. The woodland creatures vacated the forest first, gone to richer lands, perhaps; the woods grew thicker and wilder; then the dark creatures moved in, along with a darkness that could be heard, smelled, tasted, seen, felt in every fiber of a dragon's body. They all knew that things had changed, that worse would be on its way. And they had done nothing to stop it.

Blindell does not really think that eating the people would solve any problems. It would not even solve the hunger problem; most of the people in Fairendale are skin and bones, having lived through lean times themselves. But he would like to see them suffer. Suffer for his father and his mother. Suffer for the way they died, with spears and arrows in their necks. Suffer for the pain that still thrashes inside his chest when he thinks of his father's last words: "This is your home, Blindell. They may not fully trust you, but they love you. Let them."

Blindell roars, but not a dragon turns his way.

He must get out of this magic circle. He must leave the land of Morad. He must find his way to his father's people—in the north somewhere. They would welcome him. He is sure of it. And he would fit in there, among the savages his father used to bring alive in stories. They would understand his anger, his pain, his distrust. He knows it.

"Perhaps we should send a search party for Zorag." The voice of Oned shakes Blindell from his thoughts.

"He has not been gone long enough to do what needed to be done," Larus says.

Blindell would like to say, *And what is that? Mobilizing dragons to defend humans? As though any dragon would do that.* But he keeps his thoughts to himself.

"I hoped he would keep in touch, send us some sort of message to let us know how its goes," says Malera. Blindell hears the tone of sorrow in her voice.

No one says aloud the possibility that flickers through all their minds: *He could be dead.*

Blindell's chest tightens. No. His cousin is strong. He is smart. He is a king over all the other kings. He will be just fine.

"What if the man killed Zorag?" Alvah's words are soft, as though it is a secret between all of them. Blindell hears, of course; if they had wanted to keep secrets, they should not have placed his magic circle—his prison— here, where they have always assembled for their morning council.

"Zorag trusted him," Malera says. "I do not think the man will harm him."

Oh. Blindell has had enough now.

"But he is a man!" he shouts into the circle that does not include him. "He is a man, and killing dragons is what men do!" He blinks rapidly to clear his vision, to keep it dry and focused. "You cannot trust man."

"You are mistaken, Blindell," Larus says. It is the first time someone has addressed him, has seemed to hear what he has said, but the words only fan the fury.

"They killed my mother and father!" Blindell roars. "They had no reason to do it."

"He is not the man who killed your mother and father, Blindell!" This time Malera's voice is fierce, strong.

She draws herself up to her full height. The words ring out over the sandy ground of Morad. "We all lost people we loved in the Great Battle. But not all people are the king who was responsible. Not all people are the same."

Her eyes glow yellow. He is sure his are glowing deep red. He tilts his head back, opens his mouth, and releases his fire into the sky so that it does not bounce off the invisible walls of his magic circle and come back to burn him.

When he is finished, Larus and Malera are closer to him.

"Not all people want to kill dragons, Blindell," Larus says in a soft, soothing voice.

"Not all people are dangerous," Malera says in the same kind of voice.

Blindell says nothing. He hangs his head.

This is your home, Blindell. They may not fully trust you, but they love you. Let them.

Blindell's shoulders drop. His eyes blur. A wave of warmth washes over him.

And he wonders if this is love.

Plan

The question of the Grim Reaper followed Bregdon wherever he went. To the cold-packed snow of Guardia, to the sandy beaches of Lincastle, to the lovely flowered land of Fairendale. He could not escape it, just as he could not escape the Grim Reaper.

He had settled on a plan; he stalled. It was a good plan, a solid one, as far as he knew, but it would mean one final death and another rising, but different. It was not assured that the plan would work, but hope made it impossible to dismiss. After all, what else was there for him to do? The magical objects had been created, the circle of Graces completed, the magical mirror enhanced, the powerful sorcerers and sorceresses disbursed and equipped. He cast aside thoughts of Rip. Some mysteries were not made to be solved.

There was only one matter that stayed him.

Marion.

Still she wavered. He watched her eye the staff of Folen, pick it up, turn it over, search the Old Man's Great Book, linger on a Destroying spell, and set the staff back down in its corner; Bregdon whispered, "Keep it. You will need it to destroy the Grim Reaper." He did not know if Marion could hear him, but he whispered it all the same.

He watched her pacing the floor of her cottage, her face contorted as though in pain, tears rolling down her cheeks, and he whispered, "You are needed. Do not believe otherwise."

He watched her musing aloud about stealing the magical looking ball from the Graces, and he whispered, "No, my dear. It would not serve you."

She had chosen for the realm once; he had witnessed it. She had made the magical mirror, enhanced it with a Living spell (Bregdon had whispered the idea into her mind, but she had executed it expertly, without hesitation), and delivered it to Fairendale castle on the day the boy Sebastien, who would become a king, invaded the land. The bodies had disappeared; the Living spell had worked. Marion had saved.

Bregdon told himself that what he had done—all of

it—was for the best. He had worked with what he had, and he had changed things. There were the three Graces, watching over the realm. There was Kadesh, with his growing children and his happy life. There was Mira—oh, Mira. He did not want to think about Mira, who still waited for Anthony.

And there was Marion, finding her place.

Would she find her place?

Perhaps his plan would ensure it.

And the more he thought about it, the more he knew it was so.

It was a rather chilly day in the land of Lincastle—unusual enough that the people had ceased talking about the latest fashion and the new hats at the hatter's place and were discussing, instead, the strange and outlandish weather (was it caused by the mysterious rumbling of the ground that had happened days ago? The people assumed so.)—when Bregdon summoned the Grim Reaper.

"Igor Maltashah Beram, prophet of Guardia," he said. "I will you to come."

The Grim Reaper was not the only one who knew names.

It was the Grim Reaper's Black Eyed Beings who appeared first. There were many more than the last time

Bregdon had seen them. They stretched out as far as the eye could see, their eyes bottomless, the black flourishes beside their right eyes looking almost ornamental.

The Grim Reaper snarled when he flickered into being. "Who dares call me?" His voice shook the ground on which Bregdon stood.

Bregdon lifted his chin. He would not be afraid. He would go bravely into the dark night. "I do," he said, and his voice did not waver one bit.

The Grim Reaper fastened his eyes on Bregdon and tilted his head slowly, as though it pained him. But the smile on his face said otherwise. "Bregdon," he said. "I will have you at last."

It took only the barest blink before Bregdon died another death and opened his bottomless black eyes to a life much different than all the others.

The only sound in the world was the Grim Reaper's hollow laugh, echoing through the trees.

Concessions

Deep inside the Wishing Woods of Lincastle, underneath the ground in the spider lair called the Cavern of Cerata, the enormous race of Gulonon spiders is holding court. Frederick is confined in a giant spider cage—which is just like a human cage, except of magnificent proportion and with bars that are much closer together, since spiders such as himself can squeeze through the smallest of spaces. Sparso is saying that the newly hatched spider (Frederick) who is so young he does not even have a name, has already betrayed the tribe, putting them all in grave danger.

They have been seen by the people. It is forbidden.

Frederick nearly interjects that he was not, in fact, seen by the villagers; it was not until the mass of spiders came to fetch him that they were seen at all. He would have maintained his invisibility if they had not come.

But then Sparso says, "He spoke to a human," and the spiders draw in a collective gasp.

Frederick did not even know that spiders could gasp.

He cannot argue with this charge. He did speak to Miss Muffet. But it was for a noble purpose: to save her from the man who watched, the man Frederick believed was going to snatch her for his own profit. But what would spiders such as these care for the dignity of human life?

All the while he is speaking, Sparso does not look at Frederick; he merely ignores him as though Frederick does not even exist.

Frederick's heart, if he has one as a giant spider—and he thinks he does; he has felt it beating from time to time—drops into his stomach, which he is fairly certain he has as a spider, since he can feel it rumbling.

"He does not even have a name!" Sparso repeats, as though incredulous that a spider so young could wreak such havoc on an entire community.

Frederick swallows hard, to keep himself from saying more words he would like to say: He *does* have a name. It is Frederick. And he is not a spider, he is a boy from the land of Fairendale.

He catches Demarek's eyes—all eight of them—and

holds his breath, then lets it out slowly. It is something his mother taught him to do, back when she grew tired of his and Lilah's bickering.

What would his mother say to see him like this? It is a question that has haunted his days and nights since he became such a monstrous creature.

And look at them all, waiting to hear the sentence, waiting to see if they will feast on a spider tonight. He is small; he will not feed them all.

Frederick continues looking at Demarek. He feels calmer, safer, with her eyes trained on him. She will not let anything bad happen to him, will she?

Why is it he trusts her so? He cannot say.

He wonders if, after the spiders have feasted on him, he will magically turn back into a boy. He wonders if someone will deliver his body to his parents in Fairendale. He wonders if he will have a proper burial ceremony, where the spirit is set free.

He is beneath the ground of Lincastle; who would find him? Who would care to?

He will miss them all. He wishes he could have seen them again. Just once.

Frederick only hopes that the spiders will kill him humanely—before they begin their feasting.

Oh! He does not want to die being eaten by spiders.

It is the worst nightmare possible. Frederick very nearly cries out when the spiders say, "Kill him!"

Sparso, however, calls the court to order again. He says, "This spider has violated the rules of our clan." He turns to look at Frederick with all eight of his beady eyes. "But he is young. Perhaps he did not know."

The spiders are quiet, waiting. Frederick waits as well.

And then a voice rings out. "I failed to tell him the rules of our clan." It is Demarek. "He was unaware. It is my fault." Demarek bows her head. The crowd of spiders parts for her.

"Demarek," Sparso says. "Daughter." Frederick stares at the two of them. Sparso's daughter? How is this?

And how had he missed it?

Did she not say that she was a princess, that she was Frederick's sister? Which makes him…

It is impossible.

But nothing is impossible in this world, and Frederick knows it. He watches the two royals. Demarek has drawn nearer to Frederick. She looks at him and turns to her father. "Please, Father. He is only a hatchling."

"A hatchling with no instincts," Sparso says, glaring at Demarek. "A hatchling who does what he likes. A hatchling in need of discipline."

The crowd of spiders agrees with a loud, collective

murmur of approval.

"Perhaps if you let me teach him—"

"He has put us in danger!" Sparso says, interrupting whatever Demarek would have said. "Every spider here. Even you."

"It can be corrected," Demarek says. "No one is beyond the hope of correction."

The two stare at one another for a time before Sparso says, "He has violated three of our four laws. Do not speak to humans, do not let humans see you, do not venture out in daylight without permission and training."

Frederick wonders what the fourth law is. Demarek says, "He did not let a human touch him."

"Would he?" Sparso turns to Frederick, and he is aware that he must say something.

"No," he says, and then adds, "sir."

Sparso continues to stare at him. Frederick feels himself shrinking underneath the spider king's gaze. And then Sparso does something amazing. He spits a length of bright blue silk into Frederick's cage, knocking Fredericks's legs out from beneath him.

Frederick is so startled by the beautiful color of the silk that he does not mind so much the collision of his chin—if it can be called a chin—with the earth. How did Sparso do that?

And how can he see color, when he has only, so far (with the exception of Demarek's strange eyes every now and again), seen in grayscale?

Another thing Frederick does not know about these spiders is that Gulonon spiders have the ability to turn their silk whatever color they like. They are magical creatures and so have magical abilities. They envision a picture, and out comes the silk. It is an astonishing gift, considering they cannot see color. Their gift enables them to weave fantastic illusions they use to trap their prey and lead astray the humans who venture too close. He is too young to know this yet.

Sparso turns back to the throng of spiders. "Should we kill him?" he says. "And begin early on the night's feast?"

"He is very small," Demarek says. "He will not feed many." Her voice is challenging.

The spiders remain quiet, all eyes fixed on Sparso and Demarek. Sparso turns around slowly. Demarek does not flinch when his eyes flash into hers.

"I do not think you understand, Daughter." His voice is low and calm, worse, by far, than what it has been.

Demarek stands her ground, unmoved.

"We do not eat to fill our bellies," Sparso says. "We eat to teach a lesson."

"How will he learn the lesson if he is dead?" Demarek says. A few of the spiders shift. Uncomfortable or conceding the point? It is impossible for Frederick to know; he does not understand these spiders at all.

"He *is* only a baby," another spider calls out.

Sparso looks at Frederick with all the disgust that he could possibly muster. If only his face were not so human. Frederick almost starts to cry, but he thinks that this will likely enrage Sparso more. He swallows hard and blinks fast (does he blink? He cannot even tell.).

Frederick has never liked disappointing people.

"Father," Demarek says. Her voice is soft, gentle.

Sparso turns on her with raging eyes.

"No matter what you do, you will never get her back," Demarek says. "Punishing a hatchling, enforcing another law, killing all the people who may have killed my mother—it will not bring her back."

Sparso glares at his daughter, still. For one minute, two minutes, three, and then he hunches over, as though bent by the worst pain there could be in the whole world.

The spider king's eyes turn glassy.

Could it be?

And then the spider king makes a sound that begins as a hiss and turns into what Frederick assumes is a spider wail.

Evil is not born, it is made.

Perhaps his mother and the old woman with Miss Muffet were right.

Demarek moves to her father's side. She escorts him away.

Can it be over? Is it too early to hope?

The spiders begin to turn away, but something strange happens, something Frederick has seen before. A suspension of time. They all stop, half turned. Then they crumple.

"Demarek?" Frederick says. She does not answer.

Another does. It is a mellifluous voice, belonging to a woman. A voice he has heard before but cannot quite place. "Frederick," it says. "It is good to see you again."

A woman steps around the frozen spiders, a woman in a flowing green dress with eyes of the same color. Why can he see color again? What is happening?

The spiders do not move.

He is trying to understand it all when the spiders and the woman begin to grow taller, larger, and he realizes he is shrinking. Rapidly.

The Enchantress weaves through the remaining spiders separating Frederick from herself. She picks him up and says, "Much better. At least I can now tolerate the sight of you." She glances back at the spiders and cringes. "You are now a blackbird, Frederick. And safe."

With that, she places him in another iron cage, this one made for a bird, and Frederick knows no more.

There is one spider who was not affected by the spell of the Enchantress. As soon as the Enchantress and the Huntsman left the cave in which she has spent the last several days of her life, Demarek fled as quickly as she could manage (she remained a spider for the fleeing; eight legs is better than two for such purposes). She did not know how long the spells—two of them? A Freeze spell and a Suspension spell?—would last. She did not want to see what happened when the spiders learned that Frederick was gone.

Besides, she has finished her part.

At the mouth of the Cavern of Cerata, Demarek touches the band around her front leg on her right side with the front leg on her left side. The band elongates into a staff of almond-colored wood, with iron claws curling up at the top, wrapping around air. The staff drops to the floor with a muffled clatter—muffled by one of Demarek's back legs. She presses all eight spider legs to the staff, and what happens next is so strange it would be difficult to explain if one were not a sorcerer or sorceress.

Demarek peels out of her spider skin, and stands again—at last—in her former state: that of young woman with golden hair and sapphire eyes and a smooth, mostly unlined face.

The husk of the spider—which will be inhabited again by the real Demarek—falls to the ground, subject to the same spell (or spells?) that has befallen the others.

Demarek is not this woman's name. But she is a princess—a former one, at least—and that is all that needs saying.

As she turns from the body of Demarek, the woman's form flickers, and now she is a bent old woman leaning on a walking stick, white hair practically glowing in the dark. It is her favored form, so far from what she was and is that no one would even be able to guess.

Inside the woods, in a place of relative safety, the woman—for identification purposes, let us call her the Old Woman—stops. She moves her staff in a circle, and a small table appears, on which is a brown bowl. In this bowl she tosses a handful of colored stones. She studies them where they lay.

There are two green ones: the fulfillment of hope.

There is one red one: love.

There are three yellow ones: disaster.

And there is one black one: misfortune.

The Old Woman is practicing the art of lithomancy. One must ask a question before the stones are thrown, and they answer.

The question the Old Woman asked was this: What does the future hold?

The stones have given no answer, though the Old Woman fears that four negative stones mean the future is weighed with more disaster than restoration. She glances toward the direction from which she came, the direction in which lies the Cavern of Cerata. She did satisfactory work there. She achieved something for the good of the realm.

At least there is that.

The Old Woman replaces the stones in her pocket. They clank against each other until she touches her staff to the pocket, and they vanish.

She has never liked using stones, but sometimes it is necessary. An old form of magic that does not require energy.

The magic of these last several days has required much of her energy. And she has a long way to go from here.

At least she can travel quickly. She takes her staff in

hand, closes her eyes, and vanishes in a cloud of rose-colored smoke.

When she reappears, the Old Woman is inside the Weeping Woods, just outside the clearing where the house of the Enchantress sits. She sinks to her knees, hardly able to hold up her head. But there is one more thing she must do, so she draws a rectangle in front of her with the tip of her staff. What looks like a small mirror appears, and in it she sees the Enchantress and the Huntsman, talking in hushed tones inside the Wishing Woods.

"Well, I am glad to be done with that," the Enchantress says. The Old Woman can second this, but, of course, she does not. A scrying glass is unpredictable; sometimes it lets through sound and sometimes even sight. So the Old Woman hardly breathes.

"I hope the next child is human, at least," the Huntsman says.

The Enchantress says nothing. Her shoulders tense. She looks around, as though searching for something.

"What is it?" the Huntsman says.

"I feel as though someone is watching us," the Enchantress says.

The Huntsman looks around, too. They both look weary, ragged, like everyday travelers. Good. It will help their quest. The Old Woman smiles.

"I am sure we are safe here," the Huntsman says.

"You do not think the spiders will come after the boy?" the Enchantress says. "They did have him on trial." She shivers.

"It was over," the Huntsman says. His arm moves around her shoulders. "Come. You must rest a bit. I will watch over the children."

And the Old Woman will watch over them all. She will keep them relatively safe. She will see that they finish their quest, that the children are found, that the world is altogether changed by a few simple interventions.

Tonight, she will show the Enchantress and the Huntsman the next child.

Cora hunches over a dark wood desk in the corner of her sitting room. She is scribbling a letter. Every now and then she pauses, thinks, blinks her eyes to clear the blur.

She is writing to Sir Greyson. She will leave this letter rolled up at his door, wedged between the threshold and the red wood of the door. She has never trusted pigeons to deliver important letters, and, besides, she does not know where Sir Greyson is.

The first line of the letter reads, "My dear Grey."

She agonized over those first words and has, so far, begun a new letter sixteen times, over the course of four days (in actuality, dear reader, she has been stalling. Cora is a woman who moves, yes, but she is also a woman—full of hopes and dreams and, mostly, love. It is love that has stayed her departure, though she would never admit this to anyone—not even to her cat, Grimm, who has, once again, mysteriously disappeared.). But now she has written too much to stop, and so the words "My dear Grey" remain.

She uses a fountain pen that she enchanted many years ago, back when she delivered secret messages to Queen Clarion, back when the two of them were friends, back when Cora lived under the mistaken assumption that she would be a princess, that she would live in a castle, that she would be given a more privileged future. Not that she wants something like that now; what she wants, more than anything—with the exception of her magic restored—is a life with Sir Greyson, a life with her daughter, a life of fullness and joy.

Of course Cora cannot say this—not in a letter and not out loud. She writes around this truth instead.

The ink of Cora's fountain pen records the letter but disappears as quickly as it is recorded. It does not disappear forever; as soon as this letter is in the correct hands—those of Sir Greyson—the words will write themselves back across the page. When Sir Greyson has finished the letter, the words will again vanish, and no record of them will remain.

Cora has always been a careful, precise woman, even while she takes her risks.

She tells Sir Greyson that she must go on a journey. She tells him she needs her magic restored. She tells him all about having become a dragon rider, having lost her magic, having tried and tried and tried again to return the prince, whom she turned into a blackbird after stealing him from Fairendale castle, to his former form, having failed every time. She tries to keep her letter factual and crisp, but the emotions begin seeping in toward the end.

She signs the letter, "Yours, Cora."

Is she Sir Greyson's? She would like to think she is not. She would like to think that he does not deserve this letter from her, that he does not deserve to know her plans after all that he has done. After betraying her in front of the village people she used to lead. After he returned to his king—for the second time.

But she may not return. When Bree, Sir Greyson's mother, told Cora that Mages in the far north might be able to restore her lost magic, she also warned Cora that it was a dangerous quest. And Cora knows as well as anyone that the uncharted territory in the north is full of unknown dangers.

She has never allowed danger to stop her from doing what must be done.

Cora rolls up the letter and holds it in her hands for a moment. She unfolds it and stares at it again.

What if she does not return?

She dips the pen in the enchanted ink and raises her hand.

No. She cannot say it.

She drops her hand and rolls up the parchment again. She hesitates. Again.

She must. He deserves to know.

And before she can talk herself out of it, she writes, "I love you, Grey. I hope you always know that." And rolls the letter up again, stands up, and walks out her door. When she crams the letter, untidily, into the space between the door and the threshold, her vision is so blurry she can hardly see what she is doing. She stands quickly and backs away. She stares at the door for a moment, two, three, and, at last, she turns her face toward the dragon lands of Morad.

It is time to fetch her dragon and travel to the north.

To her magic. To either restoration or death.

It is worth the risk.

Calvin is inside the castle library, searching for the Old Man's Great Book, as he has been doing for the last several evenings—ever since the prophet Yerin, who is imprisoned in the dungeons beneath the dungeons of Fairendale castle along with an unknowable number of Fairendale children, told Calvin about the book, about the danger this book could pose in the hands of the monster.

His searches have ended only in frustration and hopelessness.

Where is it? He cannot let Yerin down. He must find the book. If it has information about the key that unlocks the dungeons…

But more than that: It must be kept from Yasmin.

Calvin does not understand, completely, why it must be kept from Yasmin, but the prophet was adamant about this. It is a valuable book, he said.

So Calvin continues searching. He tells himself it is for the key. He will protect the children and he will free them.

But as his search turns up nothing night after night, as the exhaustion begins to seep behind his eyes, as, more recently, Cook's leaving piles more weight on his chest, Calvin sinks into a chair. His eyes roam over the bookshelves, so many of them, stretching all the way up to the ceiling.

He is not a stranger to this library; he reads many of its books and returns them as soon as he is finished. But the problem is that there are so many books. He does not know what the Old Man's Great Book looks like, does not even know if someone has changed its appearance in order to hide it.

This is an impossible task. He does not know enough to accomplish it.

Calvin hangs his head. He should have asked the mice for help; though they are blind, they can, inexplicably, read. They would have helped him with this task. They might have more easily found the book in this massive collection of texts. But his pride got in the way. He wants to be the hero.

It was foolish to think he could be.

Calvin takes a deep breath and shoves himself out of the chair. No sense in moping. He will work. He will work until he has touched and examined and discarded every book in this library. He gazes up. It will take a very long time, but the children have access to food and water and all but the comfort of freedom.

A child should not be kept in a cage. Calvin's skin crawls. He sets to work again, with renewed vigor, thinking of the unseeing eyes of Agnes, one of the girls in the dungeons. She is brave and kind and spirited, and a dungeon has not changed that in the slightest bit, though the last time he visited two identical wrinkles of sadness had shown up around the corners of her eyes.

Calvin's chest burns.

He takes book after book after book from the shelves, hour after hour, and when his eyelids begin to drop, he has only managed the first three rows of the first bookshelf. How many bookshelves are in this room? Hundreds of them.

But he does not think about that; to think about the task before him is to give up before it has even started. He thinks about one shelf at a time. And it is in this way that Calvin moves, meticulously, up the columns and down the rows, though his eyes hardly see anything.

He will, of course, not be able to finish this task tonight. But he will try to do as much as he can.

When Calvin's eyes feel so heavy and cumbersome they begin to close while he stands, his hand resting on a book, Calvin takes a step back. He cannot be careless; he will miss the book if he is careless. He must take his time, pay careful attention.

Perhaps that means it is time to stop for the night.

Calvin puts his right hand in his pocket and feels the stone Cook—Mira—gave him before leaving him once again. It feels warm against his palm. Three days ago he tried using this stone to locate the book. It did not work. He believes this is because he had reached his daily limit. Cook said he could use the stone for three things every day, and that first day he lost count of his uses in the thrill of having, however rudimentary, the gift of magic.

He saves the stone's power now; he will need it for upkeep, work that includes cultivating a flourishing garden, protecting the castle, and maintaining the spell to break all other spells that is infused into the pot in which the king's soup is cooked. And how would he explain to Cook that he neglected the garden or, worse, let King Willis fall under the curse of the royal throne, so he could find a book? It would not do.

Calvin pulls out the stone. It is heavy in his palm, its green patch glowing, reaching into his eyes, speaking to his deepest places, whispering that he is not alone. It has the voice of Mira—or is that only his imagination?

Sleep, it says. *You are needed for many things.*

Calvin looks around the library. There are plenty of

comfortable chairs here; he does not need to walk all the way back to his servant's room to sleep tonight (he does not fancy moving alone through those dark halls, past the portraits of former kings whose eyes follow him as he passes). He can curl up in a chair.

And this he does. He chooses one of a soft green color, one that looks as though it has wings, one with soft arms. He tucks his feet and legs beneath him. A brown blanket rests beside the chair, folded into a square, and he spreads this across his body. He leans his head on one of the chair's arms.

Calvin does not sleep for long. Something awakens him, a sound of some kind or another. His eyes pop open, and he remains motionless, observing. He sees nothing. But he can feel it: a warmth spreading into the room. He stands up and moves to a table, where a strange invisible seam cuts the air in two different halves. He tilts his head and reaches out a hand.

Something is there. Something he cannot see. Something large and thick.

A book.

Could it be?

Calvin's heart thuds. He feels breathless.

He tries to wrap a hand around the invisible object, but it is much too thick. So he uses both hands to explore, and, yes, it is a book.

It is a book!

But if it is invisible, how will he know if it is the Old Man's Great Book? He does not stop to think about this. He merely picks up the book.

Or he tries to, at least. The book does not budge.

Is it too heavy for him? Calvin tries to pick it up again, but he cannot make it budge.

He swats at it, to move it, perhaps knock it off the table, but it still does not budge, and, in fact, now his hand feels as though a rock has smashed it.

"Ow!" Calvin says. He rubs his hand and glares at the spot where the invisible book remains. Or, more precisely, he glares at a spot just to the left of the book, but the book still intuits his intention.

The Old Man's Great Book is a mysterious book; at times it has a mind of its own. Those who have owned a copy say it tends to act stranger—come more alive, so to speak—the closer the day is to a full moon. Currently, it is eight days until the next full moon. The Book is wakening.

Calvin has no idea about this legend, but he senses something. He touches the book again, and this time his hand is scalded, as though instead of a book he touched a hot iron stove. Calvin glares, again, at the book—the spot just to the left of the book.

How will he get this book to the prophet if he cannot even lift it—if he cannot even touch it?

He stretches out his hand, slowly, slowly, slowly feeling for the book. He closes his eyes.

This time the book opens its pages and slams shut on his fingers.

"OW!" Calvin yelps, backing away from the table and the book. He crashes into another table, which knocks a stack of twelve texts onto the floor in a crash of sound. He winces.

What kind of game is this? He clenches his teeth and glares at the book—that is, the spot just to the left of it.

"Calvin." The voice startles him so badly that Calvin jumps, spins, and lands on the table that emptied its pile of books moments ago. His breath comes in heaves, but he is relieved to see that the voice belongs to Queen Clarion, not the monster.

"My queen," Calvin says.

Queen Clarion remains by the double doors. "Are you looking for something?"

Calvin hesitates and then says, "No, Your Majesty."

Queen Clarion's eyes are a lovely blue. Calvin meets them for a moment and glances away. He feels badly about lying to the queen. But she must know, because she says, "You have found it."

He lifts his eyes to hers, but he has no chance to answer, because the monster bursts through the doors at that exact moment.

Queen Clarion presses herself against the wall and holds a finger to her lips. The monster does not see her but heads straight toward Calvin.

"What have we here?" Yasmin says. She walks slowly, deliberately, closer to Calvin. He shrinks himself smaller, curling up on the table instead of in a chair.

Oh, he wishes he had not stayed here so long.

But he found the book.

He wills himself not to look at the table where it sits.

Calvin closes his eyes, thinking this will be easier, but then he only sees the blackness of his eyelids, and that makes Yasmin scarier, since he cannot see how close she is to him and he knows—because he is no longer a child —that closing his eyes will not make her disappear.

So he levels his gaze at her, his insides shaking.

She is not so bad; it is only the tint of her skin that makes her look monster-like. And the depth of her eyes. And the curve of her lips.

Is it everything?

No. She has beautiful hair and lashes and…

Calvin tries hard to comfort himself. He tries hard not

to look at Queen Clarion, who is still pressing herself flat against the wall. He tries hard not to scream.

The rock in his pocket grows warmer, and he is momentarily bolstered.

Yasmin is right in front of him. She lifts his chin with a finger, and he is forced to look in her eyes. They are black pools of something that he cannot name. Evil? Or simply death?

"You are in the library," she says. "You like to read, little kitchen boy?"

"Yes," Calvin manages to squeeze out of his tight throat. And then he adds, "Your Majesty."

Yasmin's laugh—low and throaty—fills the space before she says, "What are you reading?"

Calvin is not entirely sure how to answer this question. He has not really been reading, and he has never been one to whom lying comes easily. Lies make one untrustworthy, and he has never wanted to be that.

Still, he says, "I have been reading some of the stories." It is the most obvious answer he can give; this library is filled with stories. They are all stories. Every book is a story, whether it is true or not.

"And do you find them interesting? To your liking?" Yasmin takes her hand from his chin, but Calvin continues looking in her eyes.

And here is where Queen Clarion steps out from her hiding place, perhaps because she can see how uncomfortable Yasmin is making Calvin. She stands in full view, behind the monster. Calvin watches her chin lift. She says, "You have come here for a reason, Yasmin?" She does not address Yasmin by any of the proper terms for royalty. She is a queen, after all. Yasmin is nothing.

Yasmin turns on her heel, and Calvin cannot see her face, but he can imagine her smiling when she says, "Queen Clarion. Precisely the person I wished to see."

Calvin takes this moment to look at the table where the Old Man's Great Book still rests. The stitch in the air is still visible; has Yasmin seen it? He must hide it.

He scrambles off the table as silently as he can manage, while Yasmin is distracted by Queen Clarion, and he moves to the other table, standing with his back to it.

Does he look suspicious? He crosses one of his legs over the other and leans his hand on the table. No, that is worse. He folds his arms across his chest. Not much better. He climbs on the table and sits as he was.

Maybe she will believe he has not even moved.

"I am looking for a book," Yasmin says into the stillness.

Calvin's heart thumps. Queen Clarion does not even glance his way; she merely shakes her head. "There are many books here."

"This one has a name," Yasmin says. "The Old Man's Great Book."

"I have never heard of it."

Yasmin does not say anything for a long time. Calvin can imagine her eyes cutting into Queen Clarion's, but Queen Clarion does not even shift. She is the bravest woman, besides Cook, that Calvin knows.

"Well then," Yasmin says. "I suppose I will have to use your magic." Calvin feels his eyes widen. Garth told him the queen had magic, but Calvin had not believed him.

Queen Clarion confirms it with her next words: "I will not use my magic for your purposes." Her voice is low, resolute, strong. "Ever."

Yasmin stiffens. She strides closer to the queen. She says, "Oh, but you will." A pause. "If I say so."

Queen Clarion glares at Yasmin, and Calvin, though he cannot see her face, assumes that Yasmin glares right back at Queen Clarion. Yasmin reaches out a blue-hued hand and tilts Queen Clarion's chin up and back. Queen Clarion grabs at her throat, as though she is choking. Calvin tries to launch himself from the table, but fear renders him motionless. He tells himself to go, save the queen, but his body does not obey.

You see? He is no hero.

His eyes blur.

He hears a groan belonging to no one in this room. Queen Clarion and Yasmin do not seem to hear it, but Calvin knows it is coming from behind him—from the book. He wills himself to remain still.

Will Yasmin kill the queen? He must do something.

But he cannot. He is still frozen.

The queen writes something in the air, something that escapes Yasmin, that forms words behind her back. It says, *You can have the book. But you must keep it from the wrong hands.*

Calvin tries to tell the queen, with his eyes, that he understands. And he will try.

"You will come with me now," Yasmin says, removing her hand from the queen's chin. The queen rubs her neck and draws in a deep breath. "And we will leave the boy to his reading." Yasmin glances back at Calvin, and Calvin feels both a deep sense of relief and a large and looming fear. He will need to get this book to the dungeons beneath the dungeons, without Yasmin discovering him.

The queen looks at him, her gaze leveled and sure, and nods once before Yasmin flicks a hand and the queen is spun around and shoved out the door. Yasmin follows.

Calvin stares at the closed door for a time, his heart thrashing against the walls of his chest, as though it would like to escape. He breathes. He settles.

And when he has composed himself, he puts his hands on the Book, which does nothing to resist (it is a temperamental thing), and stuffs it in the front of his tunic, along with a pillow. There are bulges everywhere, but he hopes the monster will be too preoccupied with Queen Clarion to notice anything amiss.

He hopes, too, that the queen will survive whatever Yasmin has planned.

The boy was frightened. Queen Clarion can feel it, still, in her chest as she accompanies Yasmin down the hall toward the throne room. And though she, too, is frightened (never before has someone been able to turn her magic against her), Queen Clarion reaches a hand behind her and writes something else on the air, words that will fly through the library doors and spell out an important message to the boy.

She writes: *You are strong. Kind. Courageous. I know you can do it.*

She sends the message three times so that Calvin will know, without a doubt, that she believes in him, that he is capable of great things, that he is more than a kitchen boy with no family of his own. She remembers when he was brought to this castle as a young boy. His aunt and uncle did not want him, and neither did any of the families in Fairendale, at least not any of those who could afford to take him. He was a foreigner, from the land of Ashvale, and they did not want to give him a place.

He showed up at the castle, and Cook brought him into the throne room, to ask permission for securing a place for him in her kitchen.

When Calvin arrived all those years ago, Queen Clarion could see the sorrow plain in his eyes, could sense what rejection had told him about himself. Every child deserves a chance to live his best life. Kitchen boy, prince, poor, rich, foreigner, native, it does not matter.

Queen Clarion turns her attention back to Yasmin. She does not know what Yasmin wants of her, and she does not think it will be anything good. But she is strong. She has survived so much. She will survive this, too.

A burning nearly splits Queen Clarion's chest in two, but she does not cry out. Something drags her faster toward the throne room, down the red carpet, up the wooden stage, and before the throne.

Yasmin says, "And now you will sit."

Something twists Queen Clarion's body and sweeps her feet out from under her. She lands hard on the cursed throne of Fairendale.

The throne begins to glow.

Don't miss the next Fairendale adventure!
Find out what happens when a tiny girl encounters underground
creatures in Book 16: *The Girl Who Braved the Underground.*

An Interview with Frederick

Transcribed by L.R. Patton
Author

L.R.: Oh, Frederick. I am so thankful to see that you are no longer in your frightful spider skin.

Frederick: Yes. Me too.

L.R.: What did you think when you woke up as a spider?

Frederick: Well, I did not know I was a spider yet. I was in an egg sack, remember?

L.R.: Yes, I remember. And you were in there with… [shudder]

Frederick: So many spiders.

L.R.: How many do you think were in the sac with you?

Frederick: I cannot even venture to guess.

L.R.: Hundreds? Thousands?

Frederick: [shudder] Please ask me something else.

L.R.: I am sorry. It is only so strange and… horrifying.

Frederick: It still haunts my nightmares.

L.R.: I bet you never want to see a spider again.

Frederick: Never ever.

L.R.: What was it like being in the Cavern of Cerata?

Frederick: The Cavern was lovely. I never knew such underground wonders existed. Their archways—my mother would have loved them. It was only…

L.R.: The spiders? They made your time difficult.

Frederick: Yes.

L.R.: What kinds of food did you see the Gulonon spiders eat? Did you ever witness them eating a person? I am sure our readers would like to know this.

Frederick: No, I never saw them eat anything but the forest creatures.

L.R.: Oh, well. Good.

Frederick: But you know more about them than I do. Since you are the author of the story? Did you not need to research Gulonon spiders?

L.R.: Well—

Frederick: You tell *me* what they eat.

L.R.: Well, I must confess that I did not do much research on Gulonon spiders. I do not like spiders.

Frederick: Nor do I. And yet I found myself in a colony of them.

L.R.: Your only respite was your time outside of the Cavern, when you saw Miss Muffet, correct?

Frederick: Yes. Miss Muffet—I still do not know her first name—had a lovely voice, and her joy was practically contagious.

L.R.: She is a lovely girl. And do you regret what you did to help her?

Frederick: I do not know if I helped her much.

L.R.: You scared away a man who might have become her captor.

Frederick: Yes, but what happened after I was taken away by the Gulonon spiders? I never did get to know that. Can you tell me?

L.R.: Well, I—

Frederick: Did she maintain her freedom?

L.R.: Well, I am not sure I can say. We have not reached that point of the story.

Frederick: What do you mean?

L.R.: We have more story to tell.

Frederick: So you are talking to me in the future?

L.R.: Am I? So you are free from your captors as well? What did the Enchantress do with you? Did you escape the king or the Grim Reaper or whatever other forces came for you in the days and weeks after your capture?

Frederick: Oh!

L.R.: Frederick?

Frederick:

L.R.: Frederick?

Frederick:

L.R.: [sigh] Someone does not like these questions, I fear. And I forgot my vow to you—that I would start with the important questions like "Where are you now?" and "How did you escape from your captors?" before I moved on to the less important things, like what it was like in the Cavern of Cerata, surrounded by gigantic Gulonon spiders. I must apologize, dear reader; my curiosity often gets the best of me. I will try to do better next time.

If you would like to read more Fairendale extras like this, be sure to visit www.lrpatton.com/fairendale.

Farewell for now.

A Closer Look at Prophets

By Bregdon, also known as the Old Man Prophet of White Wind

Prophets play an important role in the land of Fairendale, declaring the future, warning people what might result from their actions, and, of course, expending a bit of magic when they are permitted.

Here are some things you should know about prophets.

1. Prophets have powerful magic.

That magic is restricted, however, and can only be used one day of the year—on the prophet's one hundred forty-third birthday. If a prophet chooses to use their magic that day, the magic is some of the most powerful that has ever been practiced in the world of sorcery. But because it is so powerful, it demands everything from the prophet, which means that a prophet, after using this last massive expenditure of magic, will die.

2. Prophets lose their magic when they become a prophet.

Most magical people in the world of Fairendale lose their magic when they become a parent—they, in essence, pass their gift along to the next generation. Sometimes this means the parents are somewhat old when they have children, so they have used the most years they can to practice their magic and perfect it and change things for the best and the good of all (most of them, at least). Others, however, become parents when they are younger, and these parents have the greatest chance of having their powers restored (magic restoration favors the young, though there have been some older sorcerers and sorceresses who have successfully restored their magic).

Before becoming a parent, a sorcerer or sorceress can choose to become a prophet, but if they choose to do so, they will be ineligible for having their powers restored—which is never a sure thing in the first place. As a prophet they are given the ability to See the future in varying ways and forms; some can see a day or a week in advance, some can see whole years in advance, the most powerful prophets can see centuries beyond this moment in time. But the future is also a malleable and changeable thing, so the farther ahead a prophet can See, the more likely it is that the future will change. So a prophet must use her gift frequently to ensure she has the best grasp on what is happening and what will happen.

If a sorcerer elects to become a prophet, he will only have access to magic on the day of his one hundred forty-third birthday, as mentioned above.

3. Prophets' names are important.

Prophets usually guard their full names, because with

a name comes power. If a person learns the full name of a prophet, that person can Summon the prophet anytime they wish and demand a future reading, use the prophet for their own purposes, and enslave the prophet. The name of a prophet can become a dangerous weapon in the hands of the corrupt, so a prophet guards his name at all costs. No one wants to be controlled by a master.

4. Not everyone wants to be a prophet.

Those who do not choose to become a prophet are often the younger of the magical people who are planning to start a family. They do not become prophets because there is a collection of people—called Mages, the highest of the magical order—who can restore the magical powers of a former magical person and, as mentioned before, if one is a prophet one is not eligible for this re-gifting, though I personally have known many who were worthy of it. Do you remember Aleen? Yes, well, I do, too.

5. A prophet can shape the future.

With the future he has seen, a prophet can place the right people in the right place at the right time; they can turn the tide on disaster, provided their Vision proves correct. There is a great margin of error for the Sight of a prophet, and not every prophet is equally skilled at seeing and discerning what must be done for the greatest good. There are, of course, always prophets who use their skill and gift for ill, as there are in any kind of magical or other important role.

6. A prophet must tell the future as it is.

A prophet cannot, as they say, sugar-coat a future simply because they would like to spare the one who has asked them for a Word. They can, of course, refuse to tell what they have Seen. They can strategically omit parts of it or rearrange certain pieces, but lying is not permitted. It is said that those who have, in the past, lied about their Visions spent the rest of their days unable to speak at all.

There is only one way to become a prophet: one must be chosen by another prophet. One can petition other prophets, which initiates an interview process. Most sorcerers who ask to become prophets are permitted the honor, unless there is a large infraction on the map of their past. Existing prophets are always looking for new prophets; they cannot be around forever.

If, by chance, there are no more prophets who exist in the world, there will be no new prophets. If the prophets are endangered—or, perhaps, imprisoned—the population will dwindle to dangerous numbers, which could mean the toppling of all the magical structures.

Prophets are an integral part of the magical society, and without them, much would be lost.

A Rather Lengthy Examination of the Old Man's Great Book

By L.R. Patton
Author

The Old Man's Great Book is a very important magical object in the realm of Fairendale. It is an enchanted book that contains all the spells possible in the world, including the coveted spell that can restore the magical powers of those worthy of restoration. The book, in fact, does the restoration; it does not need the spell.

The book has been sought-after by many former sorcerers and sorceresses and prophets who lost their magic upon becoming prophets (no prophetesses sought it out for power, it must be noted) as well as hundreds of sorcerers and sorceresses who never lost their magic—simply for the sheer volume of its spells inside.

What it looks like

There are many misconceptions and stories about what the book looks like—they must be set straight. It is a thick, brown book with gold patterns snaking across the leather front. A gold clasp locks it shut, and red rubies wink around its edges, though depending on who looks at it, these gems may change in mysterious ways. Sometimes those who hold the book in their hands have seen sapphires and amethysts—some have even seen diamonds.

This is, of course, part of its appeal—but heed a warning: if one tries to steal the gems from the book's cover, one will fall into a deep sleep for one hundred years, dreaming all the while of riches that will never come.

Why it is valuable

Because the book is the most complete book of spells in the realm of Fairendale, it is a coveted treasure for any magical person. It contains every spell in existence—both dark and light magic. The possessor of the book has ultimate magical power—if, that is, the possessor can locate whatever spell for which they are searching in its thousands of papery-thin pages. And sometimes the book has a mind of its own and thwarts even the best of intentions. It is a temperamental thing, said to have its own personality, which grows stranger and stronger the closer the month draws to the full moon.

The book requires a key to open it, and this key is mysteriously enchanted as well. It folds up and becomes infinitesimal and so is easily hidden by those who wish to limit access. Sometimes, if the book believes it is in the possession of the right person, the key will magically appear, dangling from the back cover. But only the observant will notice this small particle of dust, hanging by a thread. And if they do not notice, the key will disappear again, believing the possessor unworthy of taking a look inside the pages (so keep your eyes ever open).

The Old Man's Great Book is also the only known magical object in the realm that can restore the magical powers of those who have given them up to have a child or who lost them for one reason or another. One who desires to experience the restoration of magic has only to place his or her right hand on the front cover of the book, and the cover will come alive with a golden glow, illuminating the hands of all those who have used this restorative power before the current user. Each book can only restore seven magical gifts in the entirety of its existence, however, and so there are limits intended to protect the realm should the book fall into the wrong hands.

Something else that is important to note: the measure of all those magical gifts goes into the person who touches it—which is to say that if a person is the second person to touch the cover of the book and ask for the gift of magic to be restored, he will receive not only his former gift but also the measure of the person before him. The last of the seven to touch the book will receive the greatest measure of magical power—his own and the six other sorcerers before him.

I know it is all mysterious and a bit confusing; it is to

me as well, and I am the designated scribe! I am sure, as is the case with many historical items, that we do not know all there is to know about the Old Man's Great Book. Much more must be learned. But we have neither the time nor the space to examine it here.

A bit of history

The Old Man's Great Book was written, over many hundreds of years, by the prophet Bregdon of White Wind. He made three copies of the book (though most in our story know only of two). Many tried, in the years after his book entered the awareness of the people, to fabricate copies and sell them for profit. Bregdon never sold his; he had no need for money. He merely gave them away to the worthy.

In recent days the books are scattered all throughout the realm. Here are their supposed locations:

Copy 2: The castle library at Fairendale. This copy belonged to Aleen and was confiscated when she was thrown into the dungeons beneath the dungeons. She was given the copy by Bregdon himself.

Copy 1: With Marion. She was given it by Folen, who had stolen this original copy from Bregdon. (Once, before she died, Bregdon visited Aleen and urged her to recover this copy from Marion and give it, along with her own copy, to the Graces so that they alone would have the power the book and knowledge granted. But, sadly, Aleen was imprisoned and sacrificed her life for her One Last

Great Act before she could accomplish his directive. Now the directive has been lost to time.)

Copy 3: In the possession of the king of Guardia.

As your narrator, I must confess that this is not actually where the third copy is. In truth, it rests with Folen's father, Rip Van Winkle, who has been sleeping inside a cave in Guardia for one hundred years because he foolishly tried to extract jewels from the book during a moment of desperation. But that is all as it should be; this prophet's sleep ensured that Bregdon was released from his self-imposed banishment and could accomplish a great many things.

The Old Man's Great Book that lies in possession of the sleeping Rip contains within it a special message for Rip, placed there by a currently unknown person (the only clue I have gathered is that this person is a female). Upon waking, the book will speak the message to Rip. It is anyone's guess how he will feel about it.

It is said that when all three copies of the Old Man's Great Book are gathered together in one place, they will gift a sorcerer or sorceress with more magic than the world has ever seen. This is why all three copies are supposed to be given to the Graces; who knows if they will make it to their destination. This tidbit of information could also be rumor; heaven knows the people of the Fairendale realm are given to hyperbole and fantasy. One never knows if what one has heard is superstition, story, or truth.

Because of the nature of the book—it contains not only all the magical spells of the land but also necessary stories for sorcerers and sorceresses to know (such as that of the magical throne or a certain mirror inside the Fairendale castle throne room)—it continues to grow thicker and thicker, as time goes on.

As of days ago, I am told, the book stopped growing thicker.

What You Should Know About Gulonon Spiders

By Edward of Lincastle
Monsterologist

The Gulonon spiders in the Lincastle colony, which dwell in the Cavern of Cerata, believe that no humans are aware of their presence. But I am a specialist who studies monsters (a study which is, I must say, exceedingly fascinating). I know how to remain invisible when observing monsters. I have watched these spiders hunt, eat, and perform their full-moon rituals, wherein they dance and revel in their cave and make a ghastly noise inside that cannot be heard outside the cave (I know. I have observed this, too).

Here are some things to remember about these monsters.

1. They feel.

Gulonon spiders feel emotions just like humans do. The spider, Sparso, lost his wife to humans, and he feels both angry and sad about this; it is a normal human response to loss.

Perhaps that makes them a bit less monstrous?

2. They do not like the taste of humans.

Should you meet an oversized spider in the woods,

the most prudent thing to do is lie down and play dead. Gulonon spiders, despite the stories that run wild in the realm, do not like the taste of human flesh and rarely ever eat a person.

3. They run their colonies like a kingdom.

They have a king, a queen, and princes and princesses. Likewise, they also have laws in their kingdoms. The four laws of the Gulonon spiders near Lincastle are: Do not speak to humans, do not let humans see you, do not let humans touch you, and do not venture out into daylight without permission and training.

Simple enough, I think, if one is not a human caught in a spider skin.

The Royal Family of Fairendale

King Willis: The current king of Fairendale. Son of King Sebastien. Has a deep love for sweet rolls.

Queen Clarion: The current queen of Fairendale. Is underestimated by her husband and most of the kingdom, but she will prove just how powerful she is in due time.

Prince Virgil: Son of King Willis and Queen Clarion, best friend of Theo. Prefers rye bread with melted butter to sweet rolls, depending on the day. Currently exists as a blackbird, transformed by the sorceress Cora.

King Sebastien: Deceased king of Fairendale, exception to the line of boys who tried to steal thrones and were, upon failing at their quest, forever banished. Was killed by a blackbird. Now lives, as much as the dead can live, inside a magic mirror.

The Former Royal Family of Fairendale

The Good King Brendon: Former king of Fairendale responsible for the alliance between the people of Fairendale and the dragons of Morad, lost the throne when it was stolen by King Sebastien. Killed in the Great Battle.

Queen Marion: Wife of the Good King Brendon, died mysteriously when her daughter was very young. Now lives in Lincastle and is "affectionately" called the Evil Queen.

Princess Maren: Daughter of the Good King Brendon and Queen Marion. She has been missing since the Great Battle.

The Villagers of Fairendale

Arthur: Village furniture maker and magic instructor to girls who possess the gift of magic in the village of Fairendale. Is a bit reckless but always manages to come out all right on the other side—though one is not always assured it will be so.

Maude: Arthur's wife. Bakes spectacular pumpkin spice sugar cookies. Prefers caution to reckless abandon.

Hazel: Daughter of Arthur and Maude, twin of Theo. Cares for the village sheep and can even, amazingly, understand them. 12 years old.

Theo: Son of Arthur and Maude, twin of Hazel. Finishes his chores early so he can sit in on magic lessons. 12 years old. (Also known as the Huntsman, after a complicated Transformation spell turned him five years older and much ruddier than before.)

Mercy: Red-haired daughter of Cora, best friend of Hazel. Prefers spectacular acts of magic to "boring" ones.

Cora: Mother of Mercy, widow, sorceress, shape shifter with the form of a blackbird. A woman who moves. Unofficial leader of the village people in Fairendale who falls in and out of favor with them. Has become a dragon rider and somehow misplaced most of her magical powers.

Garron: The town gardener. Talks to plants as though they can hear him.

Bertie: The town baker. Enjoys showing off his air-kneading skills for the children—or used to. There is no longer much wheat with which to bake anymore.

Staff of Fairendale Castle

Garth: Page for King Willis, the oldest of twelve children. No longer calls King Willis "Your Wideness" when he is feeling particularly prickly, because he knows how dishonoring it is to call names.

Cook (Mira): One of the few shape shifters in the land. Shape shifts into a bear. Is highly annoyed by her assistant, Calvin—but not really.

Calvin: An orphan who began working as Cook's assistant after his parents died in a Fire Mountain eruption in Ashvale. He is the only one allowed through the magical door to the dungeons beneath the dungeons and so is tasked with feeding the prisoners and keeping them alive.

Sir Greyson: Captain of the king's guard. Receives medicine, which keeps his mother alive, for his service to the king. Carries a magical sword that cannot be lifted by any but him—and is the only sword that can kill a shape shifter.

Sir Merrick: Second in command to Sir Greyson. Has a blind daughter named Agnes. Disappeared in dragon fire when crossing the lands of Morad. Presumed dead.

Gus, Timmy, Florence: Three blind, talking mice. Not technically staff of the castle, but they roam about it unseen, gathering information. It is suggested they were once people, transformed by a spell.

Important Prophets

Aleen: Prophetess from the kingdom of White Wind who lived one hundred forty-three years. Wears ebony skin and what appears to be snakes for hair (though it is not). Sacrificed her life to change the fate of the Fairendale children in Book 6.

Yerin: Prophet who is one hundred forty-two years old, from the wild woodland between Lincastle and Eastermoor. Has white hair that makes the dark of the dungeons where he is imprisoned a bit less dark.

Folen: Former prophet of Lincastle, father of Iddo. Trapped in a looking glass created by Queen Marion. It was left on the grounds of Fairendale, just before the Great Battle.

Iddo: Prophet of Lincastle, son of Folen. Trained King Sebastien in both dark and light magic, though he is more scientist than sorcerer. Created a machine that can bring the dead to life again. It has only worked once.

Bregdon: Prophet of White Wind. Most powerful prophet in the land, known as the Old Man. Wrote and enchanted the Old Man's Great Book. Brought Queen Marion and the three Graces back to life. Lives life after life after life in a seemingly everlasting way.

Dragons of Morad

Zorag: King of the dragons of Morad. Wears green scales with an ivory belly. Lost his parents in the Great Battle, when King Sebastien stole the throne from the

Good King Brendon. Would like nothing more than peace.

Blindell: Zorag's cousin, raised as the dragon king's son. Wears black scales and spikes all down his back. Lost his parents in the Great Battle, when King Sebastien stole the throne from the Good King Brendon. Would like nothing more than revenge.

Larus: One of the elder dragons of Morad, male. Counselor to Zorag. Wears blue-green scales that shimmer like water. Has a green horn on the top of his snout.

Malera: One of the elder dragons of Morad, female. Counselor to Zorag. Wears bright red scales and an ivory belly.

Alvah: One of the elder dragons of Morad, female. Counselor to Zorag. Ancient dragon who has been alive since before Zorag's father was born. Wears orange scales that used to be red but have faded in time.

Oned: One of the elder dragons of Morad, male. Counselor to Zorag. So ancient he is gray, colorless, with scales peeled off in places.

Kohar: Ancient food gatherer for the dragons of Morad, male. Wears pale yellow scales.

Other Important Dragons

Rezedron: King of the dragons of Eyre, uncle of Zorag. Dying of wounds sustained from a poisonous rose in Rosehaven, believed to be dark magic.

Nischal: Rezedron's daughter. Unlikely to become queen of the dragons of Eyre, because of a law that forbids a female to inherit the throne.

Residents of the Violet Sea

Arya: Twelfth daughter of King Tritanius, who rules the Violet Sea. Adventurous, impulsive, often considered rebellious by her father. Saves the Huntsman from death by fairy magic. Loves a mortal.

Other Important Characters

The Graces: Formerly mortal women who died and were brought back to eternal life by the Old Man. Now known as Splendor, Good Cheer, and Mirth, or, collectively, the Graces. Maintain the balance of good and evil in the realm. Cannot predict the future; can only influence it.

The Grim Reaper: Master of the dead. Leads an army of Black-Eyed Beings. Longs to be seen as something more than a passing shadow.

Yasmin: Frankenstein-like creature brought back to life by the scientific tools of Iddo. Formerly known as Gladys, mother of Sebastien (future king of Fairendale, but not in her lifetime).

The lost 12-year-old children of Fairendale

Ursula

Chester

Charles

Thumbelina (known as Lina among the children)

Minnie

Jasper: Transported to the land of White Wind by Hazel's Vanishing spell. Becomes a wolf who befriends a girl in a red cloak. Runs very fast.

Frederick: Transported to the land of Lincastle by Hazel's Vanishing spell. Becomes a hideous spider who doesn't fit in and learns the cost of conformity (but fortunately does not conform).

Ruby: Transported to the land of Rosehaven by Hazel's Vanishing spell. Becomes an old woman who meets Rapunzel, befriends her, and supplies her with chamomile. She is a masterful gardener.

Martin

Oscar: Transported to the land of Lincastle by Hazel's Vanishing spell. Remains exactly the same, even down to the holes in his boots. Loves to read, steals food by pretending to be a bird, and befriends a princess (he would never admit it is, more precisely, a crush).

Homer: Transported to the land of Rosehaven by Hazel's Vanishing spell. Becomes a dwarf who can spin straw into gold, otherwise known as Rumpelstiltskin.

Anna: Transported to the land of Eastermoor by Hazel's Vanishing spell. Becomes an old, bent woman who resides in the Were Woods. Is awkward with magic, which causes some unexpected problems.

Aurora

Rose

Edgar

Harriet (known as Hattie among the children)

Isabel (known as Izzy among the children)

Ralph

Dorothy

Julian

Tom Thumb

Philip: Transported to the forest outside Lincastle by Hazel's Vanishing spell. Becomes the leader of the Merry Men, otherwise known as Robin Hood. Can shoot an arrow straight to the target, even if the arrow is crooked.

Other lost children of Fairendale

August: One of the lost boys of Fairendale, escaped with Theo. Known as the leader of the lost boys. Resides in a rundown shelter in Lincastle. 11 years old.

Leopold: One of the lost boys of Fairendale, escaped with Theo. Resides with August and the other lost boys. 11 years old.

Fineas: One of the lost boys of Fairendale, escaped with Theo. Formerly resided with August and the other lost boys, but was captured by the fairies of Never Land. 11 years old.

Norman: One of the lost boys of Fairendale, escaped with Theo. Resides with August and the other lost boys. 10 years old.

Henry: One of the lost boys of Fairendale, escaped with Theo. Resides with August and the other lost boys. 10 years old.

Ernest: One of the lost boys of Fairendale, escaped with Theo. Resides with August and the other lost boys. 10 years old.

Agnes: Daughter of Sir Merrick, trapped in the dungeons beneath the dungeons of Fairendale castle.

Blind, but quite good at hearing and sensing what others cannot.

About the Author

L.R. has never been a fan of small spiders, much less very large ones that could swallow her whole. Her sons sometimes plan practical jokes that involve plastic spiders —they always fool her, because she never stands long enough in the presence of a spider to determine if it is real or fake. Her sons never grow tired of these pranks, though she does. Very much so.

When she is not dodging fake spiders hung by string from doorways in her home, L.R. can be found jotting down poetry or notes for a new story, watching her sons with a goofy smile on her face, or hiding her face in a book.

She has written fifteen books in the Fairendale series and several books for adults and kids under the names Rachel Toalson and R.L. Toalson, respectively.

L.R. shares her castle in San Antonio, Texas, with King Ben and their six young princes.

www.lrpatton.com

A Note From L.R.

Dear Reader,

When we are staring in the face of what seems like unexplainable evil—like that of a giant spider that might want to eat us—it is very challenging to look into the eyes of the one we perceive as evil and wonder. Wonder why the person—or spider—does what he does, wonder what might have gone wrong in a life to twist it so far away from good it might never return to the baseline of the least amount of goodness expected of humanity. Wonder what we might have chosen had we grown up in that same kind of life.

Wondering, considering the circumstances around evil that contributed to the creation of it, does not excuse or dismiss that evil; it only means approaching every person—however evil we believe their deeds are—with radical empathy and compassion and the kind of love that can soak an enemy solid and let them know that they are still worthy of life and love and redemption—because they are human, just like we are.

It is a daring way to live, but it is also the most powerful way to live if we are interested in real solutions, in healing what has been broken. Our enemies (however perceived or real those enemies are) don't need our hate, they need our forgiveness, our compassion, and our love.

They need our wonder.

What will you do to promote wonder?

Reading this book, as you have done, is a good first step. I believe in a story's power to inspire, inform, multiply love, and effect real change in the lives of readers. And I write every book with this (noble, I hope) purpose in mind.

Though my writing is done alone, my world-changing is not. I need readers like you to help get my books into the hands of those who don't yet know the hope and inspiration that can be found in them. So here are some ways you can help:

1. Leave a review on Amazon.

Reviews help other readers find my books. The more readers who find my book, the better I am able to accomplish what I've listed above.

2. Tell your friends about this book.

Word of mouth is one of the most powerful tools we have for sharing the things we love—and it is, consequently, one of the most powerful tools I have for sharing my work with new readers. Your word of mouth, spread to others.

I appreciate anything you do to help my books get into the hands of readers so that love can expand and surround and make its everlasting mark.

In love,

L.R.

Acknowledgements

In the middle of writing this book I was deep in research on violence for another project I was working on. The words of so many writers—psychologists, sociologists, researchers, people who believed in the inherent worth of all people, even those who sometimes express themselves with violence—resonated with what I had seen and experienced in my own life. So my first thanks goes to them, for reinforcing what I had known all along: Evil is not who we are, it's what we do. Thank you to Peter Langman, Jonathan Fast, Philip Zimbardo, and James Garbarino for your wisdom, research, and brave storytelling.

To my husband, for having endless conversations about deep topics and engaging my passion with a passion that meets it.

To my sons, who can often be heard telling each other and friends, "You're not bad, you just made a bad decision." You are already transforming your spheres of influence, and I am so grateful to be your mother.

To my friends, who keep me going when I wonder if I can really do this.

To my God, who continues to embrace my questions with delight, who covers a multitude of bad decisions,

who continues to remind me of what to be certain and
what to leave to the realm of uncertainty—because love
is more important than judgment.

Enjoy more stories from the magical Fairendale series:

LRPatton.com/Fairendale

Starter Library

A singular obsession. A safe hiding space. A never-ending search.

The king's guard has been searching all the lands of the realm for the missing Fairendale children. But, alas, Captain Sir Greyson has returned, after many days, to report to King Willis that no children have been found. The king, quite angry at this disappointing news, orders another search, this one closer to home—right inside the dangerous Weeping Woods.

*Continue your journey into the world of Fairendale with Book 2: The King's Pursuit, a short story prequel, "The Good King's Fall" and some important bonus material, **free for a limited time.***

To get your FREE bonus materials, visit *
LRPatton.com/goodking

*Must be 13 or older to be eligible

www.ingramcontent.com/pod-product-compliance
Lightning Source LLC
Chambersburg PA
CBHW050343190726